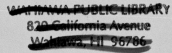

The War in Afghanistan

Arthur Gillard, *Book Editor*

GREENHAVEN PRESS
A part of Gale, Cengage Learning

GALE
CENGAGE Learning·

Detroit • New York • San Francisco • New Haven, Conn • Waterville, Maine • London

Elizabeth Des Chenes, *Director, Publishing Solutions*

© 2013 Greenhaven Press, a part of Gale, Cengage Learning

LIBRARY OF CONGRESS CATALOGING-IN-PUBLICATION DATA

The war in Afghanistan / Arthur Gillard, book editor.
   p. cm. -- (Issues that concern you)
 Includes bibliographical references and index.
 ISBN 978-0-7377-6301-0 (hbk.)
 1. Afghan War, 2001- 2. United States--Military policy. 3. United States--Relations--Afghanistan. 4. Afghanistan--Relations--United States. 5. Afghanistan--History--2001-
6. Afghanistan--Social conditions--21st century. I. Gillard, Arthur.
 DS371.412.W354 2013
 958.104'7--dc23
                       2012035628

Printed in the United States of America
1 2 3 4 5 6 7 16 15 14 13 12

CONTENTS

The US-led war in Afghanistan began in response to the terrorist attacks on the United States on September 11, 2001; attacks that took the lives of thousands of American civilians. The 9/11 attacks were planned by the international terrorist network al Qaeda and its leader, Osama bin Laden, who had been based in Afghanistan and allied with the rulers of that country, the repressive Taliban regime, since the mid-1990s. After 9/11, US president George W. Bush insisted that mullah Mohammed Omar, the head of the Taliban government, hand over all leaders of al Qaeda, and when Omar refused, the Bush administration prepared to go to war against Afghanistan.

Four distinct phases can be identified in the Afghanistan war. The focus of the first phase was deposing the Taliban regime; it involved US special forces assisting local anti-Taliban forces, particularly the group of Afghan militants known as the Northern Alliance, to overthrow the government, supported by an aerial bombing campaign led by the United States and United Kingdom. Phase one was highly successful. Within a few months of the 9/11 attacks, the Taliban had been overthrown and a new government appointed in its place.

In phase two, spanning approximately from 2002 to 2008, the focus was on defeating the Taliban militarily and rebuilding Afghan institutions and government, a process referred to as "nation building." There has been much disagreement over whether nation building in foreign countries is an appropriate role for the US military, as well as whether the effort in Afghanistan was sufficiently resourced to get that job done. Also controversial was the US invasion of Iraq in 2003, which for several years diverted significant resources from the Afghanistan conflict.

Phase two was conducted by a coalition of fifty foreign governments as well as Afghan military and security forces; of the foreign troops, the United States had by far the largest commitment of personnel and resources, as well as the heaviest casualties. Of primary concern to the United States was disrupting al Qaeda and hunting down bin Laden and other al Qaeda leaders. The United States and its Afghan allies were close to capturing Bin Laden in the mountainous caves in Tora Bora in eastern Afghanistan, in October 2011, but he escaped.

Phase three lasted from around 2008 to 2011 and consisted of efforts to counter the growing insurgency; that is, militants attempting to overthrow the democratically elected government led by Hamid Karzai and supported by the international coalition. During this phase strong efforts were made to protect the civilian population from violent attacks and to convince insurgents to give up the fight and reintegrate into Afghan society. To support these goals President Barack Obama decided to send a surge of US troops in 2009 to help quell the insurgency and protect the population.

A key event in the war occurred on May 2, 2011, when US special forces killed bin Laden, who was living in a secure compound in Abbottabad, Pakistan. Pakistan's role in the war has been ambiguous and controversial from the start. Ostensibly an ally of the United States in the war on terror in general and the Afghanistan war in particular, there have been allegations that elements of the Pakistan military and intelligence agencies have colluded with the Taliban and al Qaeda. Many al Qaeda leaders and insurgent forces have operated in and from Pakistan, particularly in the mountainous tribal regions that border Afghanistan, prompting the United States to stage attacks in Pakistan using robotic drones, leading to protest and outrage among the population of that country.

The fourth phase of the war, roughly coinciding with the killing of bin Laden to the present, involves the process of winding down the war, gradually withdrawing US troops, handing over responsibility for Afghanistan's security to Afghan police and military forces, and negotiating with the Taliban with the goal of finally achieving lasting peace and stability in that troubled land. On May 31, 2012, President Obama announced, "Today, I signed an historic agreement between the United States and Afghanistan that defines a new kind of relationship between our countries—a future in which Afghans are responsible for the security of their

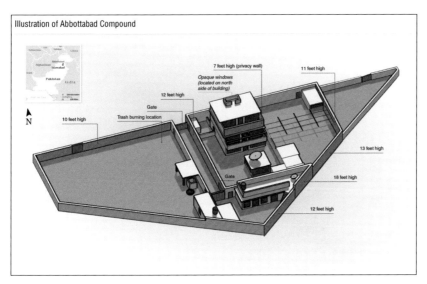

Illustration of Abbottabad Compound

This illustration shows the compound in Abbottabad, Pakistan, where US special forces killed Osama bin Laden on May 2, 2011—one of the key events in the war in Afghanistan.

nation, and we build an equal partnership between two sovereign states; a future in which the war ends, and a new chapter begins." He indicated that "by the end of 2014 the Afghans will be fully responsible for the security of their country."[1]

This has been a complex war, and the outcome is still uncertain. The conflict hasn't gone the way the original planners hoped it would. There has been much fighting in the country since US defense secretary Donald Rumsfeld announced the end of "major combat" on May 1, 2003. Certainly the United States and its allies appear to hold overwhelming technological superiority over the insurgency. Yet as Sebastian Junger, a reporter who spent a year embedded with fighters in the Korengal Valley, where the fighting was most intense, recalls,

> For every technological advantage held by the Americans, the Taliban seemed to have an equivalent or a countermeasure. Apache helicopters have thermal imaging that reveals body heat on the mountainside, so Taliban fighters disappear by covering themselves in a blanket on a warm

rock. The Americans use unmanned drones to pinpoint the enemy, but the Taliban can do the same thing by watching the flocks of crows that circle American soldiers, looking for scraps of food.[2]

The war has been costly. In financial terms it has cost the United States more than half a trillion dollars. More importantly, thousands of US and other coalition soldiers have died, along with tens of thousands of Afghan civilians. Improved medical care has led to fewer deaths but proportionately more injuries compared with previous conflicts. According to Linda Bilmes of Harvard University, "For every person who's actually been killed in this war, there are 16 wounded and injured . . . an unprecedented number. In Vietnam . . . there were 2.6 injuries for every fatality, and in Korea there were 2.8."[3]

"Every war has its own signature wounds" according to Ronald J. Glasser, a US army doctor. "In Afghanistan, it is polytrauma and traumatic brain injuries from the blasts and shock waves of car, roadside bombs, and suicide bombers that have become the major cause of casualties and death leading to what are this war's signature wounds—amputated and destroyed limbs and traumatic brain injuries."[4]

What lessons will be drawn from this war, the longest the United States has ever fought? Was it a war of necessity or of choice? What were the aims of the war, and were they achieved? Was the great cost in blood and treasure, on all sides of the conflict, worth it? The war may be winding down, with a projected end in 2014, but people will be arguing about these issues for a long time to come.

Authors in this anthology offer a variety of perspectives on the war in Afghanistan. In addition, the volume contains several appendices to help the reader understand and explore the topic, including a thorough bibliography and a list of organizations to contact for further information. The appendix titled "What You Should Know About the War in Afghanistan" offers facts about the subject. The appendix "What You Should Do About the War in Afghanistan" offers advice for young people who are concerned with this issue. With all these features, *Issues That Concern You: The War in Afghanistan* provides an excellent resource for everyone interested in this controversial issue.

Notes

1. Barack Obama, "Transcript: Obama's Remarks on War in Afghanistan," National Public Radio, May 1, 2012. www.npr.org/2012/05/01/151806990/transcript-obamas-remarks-on-war-in-afghanistan.
2. Sebastian Junger, *War*. New York: Twelve, 2010, p. 83.
3. *PBS NewsHour*, "Care for Brain-Injured Veterans Carries High Financial, Emotional Costs," April 12, 2007. www.pbs.org/newshour/bb/health/jan-june07/wounded_04-12.html.
4. Ronald J. Glasser, *Broken Bodies, Shattered Minds: A Medical Odyssey from Vietnam to Afghanistan*. Palisades, NY: History, 2011, pp. 147–148.

ONE

The United States Can Succeed in the War in Afghanistan

John Nagl

John Nagl is president of the Center for a New American Security (CNAS). He served as an armor officer in the US Army for twenty years and is the author of *Learning to Eat Soup with a Knife: Counterinsurgency Lessons from Malaya and Vietnam*. In the following viewpoint Nagl argues that the war in Afghanistan can be won because the United States and its allies now have enough resources, as well as the correct strategy, to win the conflict. According to Nagl, the robust counterinsurgency strategy adopted by the Barack Obama administration is an effective approach because it includes a combination of pressure and rewards to encourage enemy forces to reject violence and join the political process. He claims that the fact that some of the Taliban are considering political reconciliation with the Afghan government is a sign that things are moving in the right direction.

The attempted car bombing of [New York's] Times Square by a militant trained in Pakistan, occurring just a week before this week's visit to America by Afghan President Hamid Karzai [in May 2010], has refocused the attention of America and the world on the border regions of Afghanistan and Pakistan where

NATO [North Atlantic Treaty Organization] is at war with militants associated with [terrorist network] al-Qaeda. While winning in Afghanistan would not by itself defeat al-Qaeda and associated terror movements, losing in Afghanistan would materially strengthen them at the cost of many more innocent lives around the globe. And there are encouraging signs indicating that the war in Afghanistan can be won—if the international community remains committed to the fight.

The war in Afghanistan is winnable because for the first time the coalition fighting there has the right strategy and the resources to begin to implement it, because the Taliban is losing its sanctuaries in Pakistan, and because the Afghan government and the

Soldiers of the US Tenth Mountain Division and Afghan police patrol Kandahar as part of the US counterinsurgency strategy in Afghanistan. The Obama administration adopted the tactics of counterinsurgency in 2009.

security forces are growing, respectively, in capability and numbers. None of these trends are irreversible, and they are not in themselves determinants of victory. But they demonstrate that the war can be won if NATO continues to dedicate itself to the effort.

Effective Counterinsurgency Strategy

The counterinsurgency strategy in Afghanistan that the [Barack] Obama administration adopted after two policy reviews in 2009

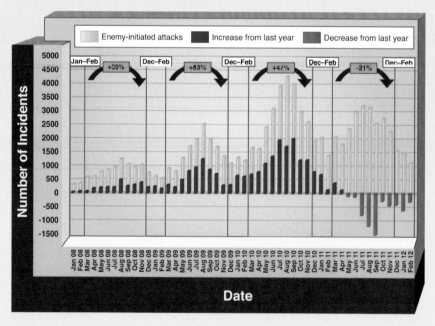

Enemy-Initiated Attacks: Nationwide Monthly Year-Over-Year Change, January 2008–February 2012

The graph shows how much change occurred in enemy-initiated attacks (EIA) compared to the same month the previous year. The light-blue bars in the background show the total number of EIAs. Red bars indicate an increase in monthly attacks compared to the same month the previous years. Dark blue bars indicate a decreased rate of attack.

Taken from: "Enemy-Initiated Attacks: Nationwide Monthly Year-Over-Year Change." NISAF Monthly Data: Trends Through February 2012, Afghanistan International Security Assistance Force, March 20, 2012. www.isaf.nato/images//20120320 _isaf_monthly_data.pdf.

is beginning to take hold. This strategy, like the one adopted in Iraq in 2007, is much more than an additional commitment of troops and civilian experts. It focuses on protecting the local population in order to provide a secure space within which political solutions to the underlying problems driving the insurgency can develop. Counterinsurgency campaigns are not won by killing every insurgent and terrorist. The most committed ideologues have to be killed or captured, but many of the foot soldiers and even the mid-level leaders can eventually be convinced through a combination of incentives and coercive pressure that renouncing violence and becoming part of the political process offer a better chance for success than continuing to fight. American troop reinforcements in south and east Afghanistan, where the insurgency is strongest, along with more effective drone strikes and an increasing Pakistani commitment to counterinsurgency, are putting more pressure on the Taliban and giving the Afghan government an opportunity to outgovern its enemies.

While an expanded international commitment of security and development forces can assist in the short term, ultimately Pakistan and Afghanistan must ensure stability and security in their own countries. The development of an Afghan government that is able to provide a modicum of security and governance for its people is necessary to ensure that the international community's security interests will be preserved without a continued major international troop presence. To achieve this objective, the coalition and its Afghan partners must build a state that reconciles a degree of centralised governance with the traditional tribal and religious power structures that hold sway outside Kabul. Achieving these minimal goals will require continued support for an increasingly capable Afghan army and much more effort in building a police force that can earn the trust of the people, as well as a greater Afghan commitment to good governance and to providing for the needs of the people wherever they live.

A Successful Outcome Is Possible

We waited until 2009 to give the Afghan conflict the resources that success will require. While we focused on Iraq, the Taliban regained strength and reinstituted its previous reign of terror in much of southern and eastern Afghanistan. But with the war in Iraq winding down and a determined international focus on Afghanistan and Pakistan, it is possible over the next five years to build an Afghan government that can outperform the Taliban and an Afghan army that can outfight it, especially with the support of a Pakistani government that continues its own efforts on its side of the Durand Line [the Pakistan/Afghanistan border]. During his visit to Washington, President Karzai discussed with President Barack Obama how the political and military efforts are faring and what endstate America will be willing to accept from Taliban negotiators, who are beginning to seek reconciliation with the Afghan government. The fact that elements of the Taliban are contemplating reconciliation is the single best piece of evidence that a successful outcome is possible in an Afghanistan that will require long-term security assistance from the West, but that with that assistance can achieve a reasonable degree of stability.

TWO

The United States Should Continue Fighting in Afghanistan

Robert Kagan

> Robert Kagan is senior fellow in foreign policy at the Brookings Institution, a public policy research organization in Washington, D.C., and the author of several books, including *Dangerous Nation: America's Place in the World from Its Earliest Days to the Dawn of the 20th Century* and *The World America Made*. In the following viewpoint Kagan argues that the United States needs to maintain a strong war effort in Afghanistan because the conflict is vital to US security interests. He claims that the Barack Obama administration is reducing the US commitment to the war for political reasons and that this is undermining military strategic needs to maintain a strong presence there. Kagan disagrees that the cost of the war is undermining domestic needs in the United States, asserting that a resurgence in terrorism facilitated by a premature US withdrawal would be far more costly to the United States than continuing a strong military campaign in Afghanistan.

"America, it is time to focus on nation building here at home." This was the core sound bite in President [Barack] Obama's speech [on June 22, 2011,] announcing the drawdown of forces in Afghanistan, and it was an extraordinary statement. Of course,

In a televised address to the nation on June 22, 2011, President Barack Obama announces his plan to reduce the number of US troops in Afghanistan.

such sentiments have been uttered many times over the years. [US senator] George McGovern's "Come Home America" campaign theme in 1972 comes to mind, and we're sure [conservative commentator] Patrick Buchanan, [libertarian Texas congressman] Ron Paul, [Ohio Democratic congressman] Dennis Kucinich, and [conservatice journalist] George Will have said either exactly that or something similar at one time or another.

Not since the 1930s has an American president struck such an isolationist theme in a speech to the American people, however. By juxtaposing the winding down of the war in Afghanistan with the need to focus on domestic problems, Obama gave presidential sanction to the erroneous but nevertheless widespread belief that whatever the United States does abroad detracts from our ability to address our problems at home. We wonder if the speechwriters, policymakers, and of course the president himself fully understood the damaging effect such a statement can and probably will have on the entire scope of American foreign and defense policy.

We can imagine that line being thrown back in the administration's face the next time it comes to Congress to defend the foreign aid and defense budgets, the intervention in Libya, or the forward deployment of U.S. forces in Asia and Europe. But maybe Obama's increasingly evident concern about winning reelection trumped such issues. Maybe the cheap shot—with its clear implication that the efforts of our military in Afghanistan actually detract from the nation's well-being—was too good to pass up.

Failure Would Be Costly

And it is a cheap shot. Here's the core point that Ron Paul, Dennis Kucinich, George Will, and now Barack Obama can't quite seem to understand: Failure in Afghanistan will cost much, much more than the billions spent on this surge. What was the cost to the U.S. economy of the attacks on 9/11? What will be the cost if the terrorist groups now operating in Afghanistan—the Haqqani network, Lashkar-e Taiba, as well as al Qaeda—are able to reconstitute safe havens and the next president has to send troops back in to clear them out again? It is a peculiar kind of wisdom that can only see the problems and costs of today and cannot imagine the problems and costs of tomorrow.

The argument that the cost of the surge in Afghanistan undermines our ability to address our domestic problems is especially risible [laughable] coming from this president. It would be one thing if cutting back in Afghanistan were part of a sweeping deficit-reduction plan where domestic programs and entitlements were getting the axe, too. It would still be a mistake. But at least it would be consistent.

There is something appallingly cynical, however, in this president suggesting that the American fiscal crisis required overruling his military leadership and ordering a more rapid and therefore more dangerous drawdown in Afghanistan—this, after two and a half years of proposing spending on domestic programs that dwarfs the cost of the surge.

Undermining Military Strategy

We're glad to see no one is contesting the fact that the president overruled the unanimous advice of his military leadership in ordering this drawdown. Yes, our military leaders have saluted and "endorsed" the president's plan. But they make no secret of their opposition to it. This is especially true of the September 2012 deadline. Where did that date come from? It must have come from Obama campaign headquarters in Chicago because, while we can see a political reason for wanting those troops out before voters go to the polls in November 2012, there is no military or strategic justification whatsoever. In Obama's new plan, the forces will be withdrawing right in the middle of the fighting season.

General David Petraeus and his commanders wanted to get two more full fighting seasons in before ending the surge. This year [2011] they are battering and pushing back the Taliban and the terrorists from the southern and central parts of Afghanistan. Next year their goal was to push them out of the eastern parts of Afghanistan. Now that effort has been cast into serious doubt. The result may be continued safe havens for the enemy, allowing them to begin attacking again in the areas cleared out this year by the surge. The difference between Obama's politically motivated strategy and the commanders' military strategy could well prove the difference between success and failure.

The psychological effect of Obama's announcement may be just as damaging. The tone of the speech, the war-weariness it exhibited, combined with the unexpectedly rapid drawdown, will convince everyone in the region, and everyone in the world, that

Twenty-Five Most Costly Insured Catastrophes Worldwide, 1985–2010

The terrorist attack on the United States on September 11, 2001, was the second-most costly catastrophe between 1985 and 2010—and the only one of the top twenty-five that was not caused by an earthquake or storm.

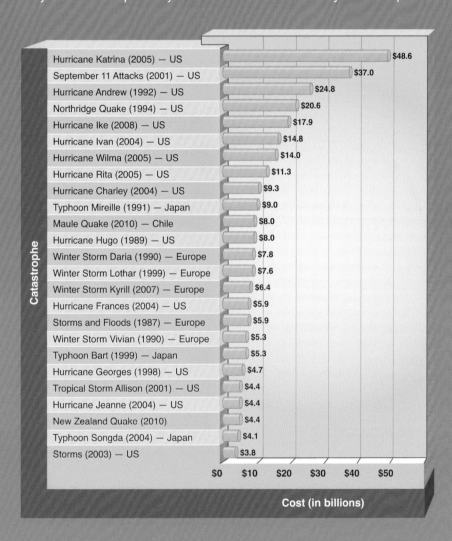

the United States can't wait to get out, regardless of the consequences. Afghan civilians who have to decide what's safest, sticking with the Americans or giving in to the Taliban, will be increasingly unlikely to choose the Americans. Taliban fighters trying to decide whether it might be a good idea to lay down their weapons before being crushed by an inevitable American victory will now view that victory as anything but inevitable. Bad actors in Pakistan, who have always doubted America's staying power, will now feel confident that we are leaving fast and will act accordingly. Our European allies, who were barely hanging on in Afghanistan in any case, will no doubt trip over themselves in a rush to the exits. They have "nation-building" to do at home, too.

Dangerous Times for the United States

And although this decision was clearly made for political reasons, the irony is that it is likely to backfire. If the war does not look like it is going well next spring and summer [2012], as troops are being prematurely withdrawn, Obama will take the blame. Everyone will know that he overruled his military advisers to formulate this plan. Everyone will know he did it for political reasons. Obama will own it. And the thing is, there will still be 70,000 American troops in Afghanistan—only at that point, instead of being part of a winning effort, they could well be part of a losing effort. Oh, to be the Republican nominee in that scenario!

Which brings us to the Republicans. They have not all covered themselves in glory this week [early July 2011]. Some have been stalwarts in opposing the president's plan, and for the right reasons. But some have been cautious, evidently worrying about the same polls that Obama is worrying about.

That is a mistake. It is a mistake in the most fundamental sense that losing in Afghanistan is profoundly not in America's interest, and every Republican has an obligation to place national interests above party and personal ambition. But it is also a political mistake. We know the conventional wisdom is that this election will be won on the economy. That may be mostly true, but we are confident that it is not entirely true. The next two years are going to continue to be dangerous times for the United States and for our friends and allies around the world. Indeed, they may be more dangerous than the past few years.

The Middle East is in turmoil. Yemen may be collapsing and could become a base for a very dangerous terrorist organization, Al Qaeda in the Arabian Peninsula. The United States may well have to use force to address that danger. Regimes in the Arab world are toppling, and it is unclear what will replace them.

China grows stronger. Russia grows more authoritarian. Iran may be close to acquiring a nuclear weapon. We could go on.

The point is that 2012 will be an election about the economy, but it will also be an election about national security. The American people may tell pollsters they want to focus on domestic problems—they have said that many times in the past, as well—but they will also be looking to see who can be a reliable and strong commander in chief. Me-too-ing Obama or, worse, trying to outflank him on the dovish left will not serve any candidate well in the general election. National security until now has been a Republican advantage. To squander that advantage in these times of global danger would be worse than a blunder. It would be a crime.

THREE

The United States Should End the War in Afghanistan

Eugene Robinson

> Eugene Robinson is a Pulitzer Prize–winning columnist with the *Washington Post*. In the following viewpoint Robinson argues that the United States has achieved as much as it can in Afghanistan and therefore it is time to "declare victory and leave." He claims that as of the summer of 2011 the United States had already accomplished its goals for the war: overthrowing the Taliban regime, destroying al Qaeda's infrastructure, and killing Osama bin Laden, the mastermind behind the attacks on the US on September 11, 2001. The author claims that the cost of continuing the war in Afghanistan—both financially and in the lives of United States soldiers—would not be worth any further gains that might be achieved. According to Robinson, Afghanistan is not likely to be any more secure if the United States stays until the planned withdrawal in 2014, and suggests ending the war now.

Slender threads of hope are nice but do not constitute a plan. Nor do they justify continuing to pour American lives and resources into the bottomless pit of Afghanistan.

Ryan Crocker, the veteran diplomat nominated by President [Barack] Obama to be the next U.S. ambassador in Kabul, gave a realistic assessment of the war in testimony Wednesday [June 8, 2011,] before the Senate Foreign Relations Committee. Here I'm using "realistic" as a synonym for "bleak." Making progress is hard, Crocker said, but not hopeless.

Not hopeless.

What on earth are we doing? We have more than 100,000 troops in Afghanistan risking life and limb, at a cost of $10 billion a month, to pursue ill-defined goals whose achievement can be imagined, but just barely?

The US ambassador to Afghanistan, Ryan Crocker, gives testimony before the Senate Foreign Relations Committee on US progress in the Afghan war.

International Terrorism Is Mobile

The hawks tell us that now, more than ever, we must stay the course—that finally, after Obama nearly tripled U.S. troop levels, we are winning. I want to be fair to this argument, so let me quote Crocker's explanation at length:

> What we've seen with the additional forces and the effort to carry the fight into enemy strongholds is, I think, tangible progress in security on the ground in the South and the West. This has to transition—and again, we're seeing a transition of seven provinces and districts to Afghan control—to sustainable Afghan control. So I think you can already see what we're trying to do—in province by province, district by district, establish the conditions where the Afghan government can take over and hold ground.

Sen. Jim Webb, D-Va., a Vietnam veteran and former secretary of the Navy, pointed out the obvious flaw in this province-by-province strategy. "International terrorism—and guerrilla warfare in general—is intrinsically mobile," he said. "So securing one particular area . . . doesn't necessarily guarantee that you have reduced the capability of those kinds of forces. They are mobile; they move."

The United States Has Done What It Can

It would require far more than 100,000 U.S. troops to securely occupy the entire country. As Webb pointed out, this means we can end up "playing whack-a-mole" as the enemy pops back up in areas that have already been pacified.

If our intention, as Crocker said, is to leave behind "governance that is good enough to ensure that the country doesn't degenerate back into a safe-haven for al-Qaeda," then there are two possibilities: Either we'll never cross the goal line, or we already have.

According to Obama's timetable, all U.S. troops are supposed to be out of Afghanistan by 2014. Will the deeply corrupt, frustratingly erratic Afghan government be "good enough" three years from now? Will Afghan society have banished the pov-

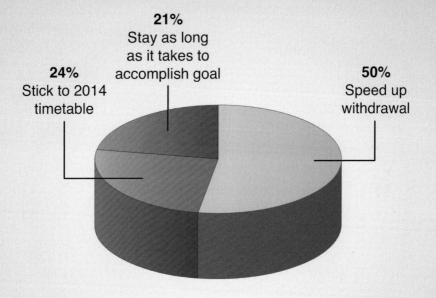

The United States plans to withdraw its troops from Afghanistan by the end of 2014. Which would you prefer?

21%
Stay as long
as it takes to
accomplish goal

24%
Stick to 2014
timetable

50%
Speed up
withdrawal

Note: Margin of error ±4 percentage points.

Taken from: Susan Page. "Poll: Half of Americans Back Faster Pullout from Afghanistan." *USA Today*, March 14, 2012. www.usatoday.com/news/washington/story/2012-03-14/poll-afganistan-pullout/53529896/1.

erty, illiteracy and distrust of central authority that inevitably sap legitimacy from any regime in Kabul? Will the Afghan military, whatever its capabilities, blindly pursue U.S. objectives? Or will the country's civilian and military leaders determine their self-interest and act accordingly?

Democrats on the Senate Foreign Relations Committee issued a report this week [mid-June 2011] warning that the nearly $19 billion in foreign aid given to Afghanistan during the past decade may, in the end, have little impact. "The unintended consequences of pumping large amounts of money into a war zone cannot be underestimated," the report states.

Declare Victory and Leave

The fact is that in 2014 there will be no guarantees. Perhaps we will believe it incrementally less likely that the Taliban could regain power and invite al-Qaeda back. But that small increment of security does not justify the blood and treasure that we will expend between now and then.

I take a different view. We should declare victory and leave.

We wanted to depose the Taliban regime, and we did. We wanted to install a new government that answers to its constituents at the polls, and we did. We wanted to smash al-Qaeda's infrastructure of training camps and safe havens, and we did. We wanted to kill or capture Osama bin Laden, and we did.

Even so, say the hawks, we have to stay in Afghanistan because of the dangerous instability across the border in nuclear-armed Pakistan. But does anyone believe the war in Afghanistan has made Pakistan *more* stable? Perhaps it is useful to have a U.S. military presence in the region. This could be accomplished, however, with a lot fewer than 100,000 troops—and they wouldn't be scattered across the Afghan countryside, engaged in a dubious attempt at nation-building.

The threat from Afghanistan is gone. Bring the troops home.

FOUR

The Counterinsurgency Strategy in Afghanistan Is Succeeding

Frederick W. Kagan and Kimberly Kagan

> Frederick W. Kagan is resident scholar and director of the Critical Threats Project at the American Enterprise Institute. Kimberly Kagan is president of the Institute for the Study of War. In the following viewpoint the authors argue that the counterinsurgency strategy in Afghanistan has a proven track record. The Kagans say that throughout 2010 and 2011, the counterinsurgency efforts were highly successful in southern Afghanistan, where General Stanley McChrystal focused the counterinsurgency resources he had been given. The authors claim that eastern Afghanistan has a stronger insurgency because not enough resources were available in that area to wage a fully successful campaign. According to the Kagans, the United States needs to continue the counterinsurgency strategy that has proven successful both in Iraq and in southern Afghanistan and to devote sufficient resources long enough for it to succeed throughout the country.

U.S. and allied forces have made great progress in Afghanistan since the start of the counterinsurgency campaign in early 2010. But critical military tasks remain—and these can only be accomplished by a substantial deployment of U.S. troops. Last

May [2011], U.S. President Barack Obama announced that he would be withdrawing 10,000 U.S. troops before the end of 2011 and the remaining 20,000 surge troops by September 2012, leaving a total of 68,000 in the country. He tabled further decisions on force levels prior to 2014, at which time Afghanistan will take full responsibility for its own security, according to the framework that NATO [North Atlantic Treaty Organization] and Afghanistan established in Lisbon [Portugal] last November. The rapid dialing back of the surge is a risky strategy, though if executed correctly, and not rushed, it is workable.

Some members of the Obama administration, along with experts such as retired General David Barno and the journalist Linda Robinson, have recommended that Obama end the counterinsurgency mission next year and refocus U.S. troops on supporting the Afghan security forces. But that is a recipe for failure. Accelerating the drawdown and ending the counterinsurgency mission sooner than planned would not only squander the valuable gains made over the last two years but prevent both U.S. and Afghan forces from engaging decisively against insurgent and terrorist groups that threaten the security of Afghanistan, Pakistan, and the United States.

Favorable Counterinsurgency Outcomes

Enemies determined to kill U.S. citizens and rebuild sanctuaries remain in Afghanistan. Insurgent groups closely affiliated with al Qaeda—such as the Pakistani Taliban, Lashkar-e-Taiba, and the Islamic Jihad Union of Uzbekistan—still have safe havens in eastern Afghanistan. Afghan security forces will not be able to eliminate those territories on their own, because they do not (and will never) have the sophisticated, high-end capabilities needed to conduct intelligence-driven, combined-arms operations in the mountainous terrain surrounding the capital and the populated areas along the roads. Even Washington's NATO allies generally lack the capability to execute combined-arms tasks, so it is unreasonable to expect the Afghans to acquire these skills, especially on such a short timetable. If American troops do not clear these

Total civilian casualties in Afghanistan were significantly lower in January–February 2012 compared to the same time the previous year. Casualties caused by the International Security Assistance Force (ISAF)—the United States and its allies—declined by 77 percent in that period, which also saw a significant reduction in civilian casualties caused by insurgents.

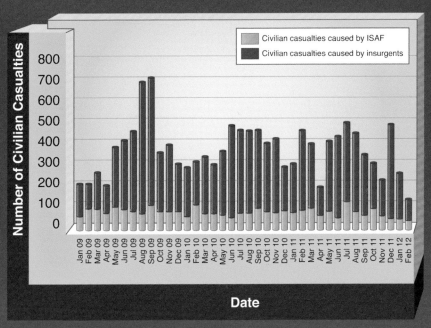

Taken from: Afghanistan International Security Assistance Force. "Monthly Civilian Casualties with Assigned Culpability." ISAF Monthly Data: Trends Through February 2012, March 20, 2012. www.isaf.nato.int/article/news/monthly-trends.html.

safe havens, no one will. Over time, they will permit terrorists to operate more freely in Afghanistan, threatening the United States and its allies in the region and in Europe, where a number of groups based on the Afghanistan-Pakistan border have cells.

A continued counterinsurgency campaign would allow the United States, NATO, and Afghan forces to work side by side in reducing the capacity, coherence, and reconstitution of enemy groups while bringing greater government control to populated areas. Consider the real gains made in Helmand and Kandahar provinces in southern Afghanistan. Over the last two years [2010–2011], U.S., allied, and Afghan troops eliminated all of the strategically significant insurgent safe havens. They cleared the traditional Taliban strongholds, including those west of Kandahar that had seen the emergence of the Taliban movement and Mullah Omar in the 1990s. Now, the troops are in the process of establishing a combination of Afghan uniformed police, national army officers, and local police to ensure that insurgents cannot regain control of cleared areas. The fighting season of 2012 will be the acid test for that effort, but the indicators so far are positive.

Afghan policemen take part in military training at a police camp in Afghanistan. The NATO coalition is in the process of establishing a combination of Afghan uniformed police, army officers, and local police in an attempt to ensure that insurgents cannot regain control of liberated areas.

More Resources Needed

Now, look east. U.S. and Afghan forces have been starved for combat power in eastern Afghanistan, even during Obama's 2009 surge; he did not fully resource General Stanley McChrystal's requests, sending only about 75 percent of the troops the general asked for. Consequently, McChrystal concentrated the reinforcements in the south rather than dispersing them thinly throughout the entire Pashtun belt. By shortchanging requests from his commanders, Obama effectively extended the time it would take to execute a successful counterinsurgency campaign, then he backed an even shorter timetable for withdrawal.

The east remains a significant threat not only to a viable government in Kabul but also to U.S. interests as well. Insurgents in eastern Afghanistan belong to various groups—the al Qaeda–linked Haqqani network is predominant, but groups reporting directly to Mullah Omar and to the Hezb-e-Islami group led by Gulbuddin Hekmatyar, have a significant presence. And south of Kabul, Taliban safe havens persist in both rural and populated areas close to small cities and highways with access to the capital and international airports. Neither the coalition nor the Afghan forces have ever had the resources necessary to clear such delimited and long-standing safe havens in Ghazni, Khost, Logar, Paktia, and Wardak provinces. Efforts in 2011 have eliminated or contained some—particularly near Kabul—but many still remain.

Successful Counterinsurgency

There is a workable solution to eliminate enemy safe havens while restricting counterinsurgency operations to populated areas. Konar province offers a glimpse of the balanced effort that would be required across eastern Afghanistan. A mélange of insurgent and terrorist groups retain limited and generally isolated sanctuaries among the 10,000-foot mountains. But U.S. and Afghan forces have secured only the populated major valleys while conducting targeted strikes into the hinterland to ensure that isolated safe havens there do not become operationally or strategically dangerous.

But it takes U.S. troops to get this done, especially in the areas south of Kabul that are more populated and central than Konar and thus less suited to targeted strikes. The insurgent safe havens south of Kabul are too established, dispersed, and well situated on the terrain for Afghan security forces to clear them alone. Support from sanctuaries in nearby North Waziristan [Pakistan] is very important for these groups. Insurgents, particularly along the ring road south of Kabul, have resilient local support networks that would endure even if backing from Pakistan came to a halt. The pattern of counterinsurgency success learned in Iraq, and now in southern Afghanistan, is proven. U.S. troops clear insurgent strongholds, then Afghan forces hold them against enemy attempts to re-infiltrate them. Throughout, both U.S. special operations forces and, increasingly, their indigenous partners conduct raids and strikes against particular network leaders.

In war, as in so many things, the devil is in the details. The question facing the United States today is not whether the troops will come home but precisely when and with what consequences. Obama's current drawdown plan risks failure by making it more difficult for both coalition and Afghan security forces to sustain gains in the south; accelerating that plan would make its problems even worse. Should Obama move too hastily, he will fail to achieve the basic objectives he laid out in his own strategy.

FIVE

The Counterinsurgency Strategy Cannot Succeed in Afghanistan

Gian P. Gentile

Gian P. Gentile is a currently serving army officer with a doctorate in history from Stanford University. In 2006 he commanded a combat battalion in west Baghdad. In the following viewpoint Gentile argues that the counterinsurgency strategy being pursued in Afghanistan will not succeed because it is being mistakenly used to attempt nation building (creating a stable, well-functioning government presiding over a people with a strong sense of national identity). Gentile says that while it would be theoretically possible to build a nation in Afghanistan by military means, US society would not be willing to spend the time and resources it would take to achieve it. According to the author, the true mission the military has been given is that of defeating al Qaeda in Afghanistan and Pakistan so that the terrorist group cannot launch attacks against the United States (often called a "counterterrorism" strategy). That goal is achievable, Gentile claims, but the strategy of nation building through counterinsurgency is not.

The problem in Afghanistan isn't poor generalship, nor is it any uncertainty about the basics of counterinsurgency doctrine by the US Army and the US Marines—they "get it." Better generals in Afghanistan will not solve the problem. The recently relieved [on June 23, 2010,] commander in Afghanistan, Gen. Stanley McChrystal, was put in place because he was the better general of counterinsurgency, sent there to rescue the failed mission. Now we've placed our hopes in an even better general, his successor, Gen. David Petraeus.

No One Can Do the Impossible

But no one, no matter how brilliant, can achieve the impossible. And the problem in Afghanistan is the impossibility of the mission. The United States is pursuing a nation-building strategy with counterinsurgency tactics—that is, building a nation at the barrel end of a gun.

Might armed nation-building work in Afghanistan? Sure, but history shows that it would take a very, very long time for a foreign occupying power to succeed. Are we willing to commit to such a generational effort, not just for mere months or years?

The US military tried to do nation-building in Vietnam with major combat forces from 1965 to 1972. It failed because that mission was impossible, too. Muddled strategic thinking, however, caused Washington to commit to a major military effort in South Vietnam when its vital strategic interests did not demand such a maximalist effort. The war was simply not winnable based on a moral and material cost that the American people were willing to pay. Yet once Washington committed itself to Vietnam, it failed to see in the closing years that the war was lost. Instead it doggedly pursued an irrelevant strategy that got thousands more US soldiers killed.

Afghanistan today eerily looks more and more like Vietnam.

Alternatives to Nation-Building

There are alternatives to nation-building in Afghanistan. Columbia University scholar Austin Long recently offered an

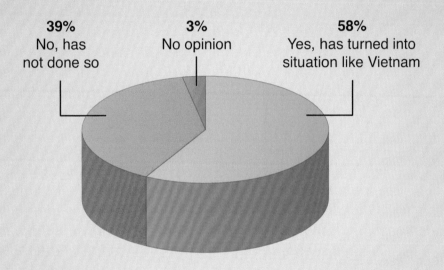

Percent of Americans Who Compare Afghanistan War to Vietnam War

A CNN/ORC poll in October 2011 asked, "Do you think the war in Afghanistan has turned into a situation like the United States faced in the Vietnam War, or don't you think so?"

39%
No, has
not done so

3%
No opinion

58%
Yes, has turned into
situation like Vietnam

Taken from: CNN/ORC poll, October 14–16, 2011. http://i2.cdn.turner.com/2011/images/10/28/re/17h.pdf.

operational method that would reduce significantly the size of the US military in Afghanistan by transforming its mission from building up Afghan society to destroying and disabling Al Qaeda, along with limited training and advising to the Afghan military. This smaller force would focus on the areas most likely to harbor potential links and alliances with Al Qaeda.

Unfortunately, Washington is caught in a cycle of thinking that sees each setback in the war in Afghanistan as a failure of the US military. Such thinking tends to exacerbate bad policy.

Petraeus often used the phrase "hard is not hopeless" when referring to the challenges he faced in Iraq during the troop surge in 2007. To be sure, at the tactical level the values of persistence, positivism, and strength of will are essential qualities for an army and its leaders.

But at the level of strategy, where military operations should be linked to achieving policy objectives, sometimes the qualities of subtleness, reflection, and flexibility are needed. A good strategist will recognize whether the military means are sufficient and proper to achieve the desired political ends.

Defeating Al Qaeda Is the Objective

President Obama has given the American military the mission of disrupting, dismantling, and defeating Al Qaeda in Afghanistan and Pakistan so that it cannot carry out strikes against the US from those locations. Contrary to common belief, this is a limited policy objective. Yet US military leaders have embraced the president's limited objective expansively by attempting to reconstruct governments and reshape entire societies. Here is a serious mismatch between a limited political objective and the method employed to achieve it.

History offers examples of policy objectives being matched with good military strategy. In one of the most brilliant and far-sighted acts of statesmanship in the 20th century, French President Charles de Gaulle decided in 1961 to withdraw French troops from Algeria and grant that country its independence from French colonial rule. De Gaulle's decision was anything but easy. He faced stinging political and military criticism, doomsday predictions about the consequences of abandoning Algeria, and an attempted military coup. Nonetheless, he recognized that staying in Algeria was destroying the French Army and dividing French society. It had become an impossible mission for France.

Dangers of Selective Reflection

Afghanistan is to America in 2010 what Algeria was to the French in 1961. Yet instead of accepting the impossibility of nation-building in Afghanistan and adjusting accordingly, the US Army and the greater defense establishment continue to see

General David Petraeus was appointed commander in Afghanistan in June 2010.

the problem not in the impossibility of the mission but in its own inability to carry out the tactics of the mission on the ground. The answer, the solution, the key to victory rests with us and what we do or don't do.

So the thinking goes: If things don't progress accordingly, senior generals can be quickly removed for not applying correctly the proper principles of counterinsurgency and nation-building.

Or the Army can be labeled a failure due to its so-called institutional resistance to fighting irregular wars of counterinsurgency.

Such selective reflection—the kind that fails to question the premise of the mission—sets the stage for a future round of "new and improved" (yet still futile) effort: The Army finds better methods for building schools and bridges in the flatlands of Kandahar or the mountains of the Hindu Kush, and with fresh generals supercharged with expert advice, it feels confident of success and even victory. And then if success doesn't happen, the cycle kicks in again: Blame the US military and its generals but then offer the hope that future success rests with us.

But imagine the possibility that the US Army and its generals at this point after eight years and more of counterinsurgency warfare in Iraq and Afghanistan actually do understand the basics of counterinsurgency and nation-building and are reasonably proficient at it on the ground in Afghanistan. Then what? Where do analysts and experts and even military officers turn to place the blame for lack of progress in Afghanistan?

By focusing on the American military and the promise of better tactical methods and generals, we neglect the true nature of the impossibility of nation-building at the barrel of a gun in the graveyard of empires.

SIX

1 Soldier or 20 Schools?

Nicholas D. Kristof

Nicholas D. Kristof is a two-time Pulitzer Prize–winning columnist for the *New York Times* and coauthor of *Half the Sky: Turning Oppression into Opportunity for Women Worldwide*. In the following viewpoint Kristof argues that spending money on education in Afghanistan would be a much better use of US resources than spending money to fight a war there. The author cites various statistics supporting his claim that the United States is spending a disproportionate amount of money on war. According to Kristof, the amount of money that it costs to have one US soldier fighting in Afghanistan could start twenty schools there. He says the humanitarian organization CARE (Cooperative for Assistance and Relief Everywhere) runs 300 schools in Afghanistan, and Greg Mortenson's Three Cups of Tea project has founded another 145 schools in Afghanistan and Pakistan. Kristof says the fact that none of those schools has been destroyed by the Taliban shows that military protection is not needed to support education there, as some people claim.

Nicholas D. Kristof, "1 Soldier or 20 Schools?" *New York Times*, July 29, 2010, pp. A29. Copyright © 2010 by New York Times. All rights reserved. Reproduced by permission.

The war in Afghanistan will consume more money this year alone than we spent on the Revolutionary War, the War of 1812, the Mexican-American War, the Civil War and the Spanish-American War—combined.

A recent report from the Congressional Research Service finds that the war on terror, including Afghanistan and Iraq, has been, by far, the costliest war in American history aside from World War II. It adjusted costs of all previous wars for inflation.

Those historical comparisons should be a wake-up call to President Obama, underscoring how our military strategy is not only a mess—as the recent leaked documents from Afghanistan suggested—but also more broadly reflects a gross misallocation of resources. One legacy of the 9/11 attacks was a distortion of American policy: By the standards of history and cost-effectiveness, we are hugely overinvested in military tools and underinvested in education and diplomacy.

It was reflexive for liberals to rail at President George W. Bush for jingoism. But it is President Obama who is now requesting 6.1 percent more in military spending than the peak of military spending under Mr. Bush. And it is Mr. Obama who has tripled the number of American troops in Afghanistan since he took office. (A bill providing $37 billion to continue financing America's two wars was approved by the House on Tuesday and is awaiting his signature.)

Under Mr. Obama, we are now spending more money on the military, after adjusting for inflation, than in the peak of the cold war, Vietnam War or Korean War. Our battle fleet is larger than the next 13 navies combined, according to Defense Secretary Robert Gates. The intelligence apparatus is so bloated that, according to *The Washington Post*, the number of people with "top secret" clearance is 1.5 times the population of the District of Columbia.

Meanwhile, a sobering report from the College Board says that the United States, which used to lead the world in the proportion of young people with college degrees, has dropped to 12th.

What's more, an unbalanced focus on weapons alone is often counterproductive, creating a nationalist backlash against foreign

Students attend class at Habibia High School in Kabul. Proponents of more education in Afghanistan say the money spent on maintaining one soldier in the country for one year could be used to build twenty new schools.

"invaders." Over all, education has a rather better record than military power in neutralizing foreign extremism. And the trade-offs are staggering: For the cost of just one soldier in Afghanistan for one year, we could start about 20 schools there. Hawks retort that it's impossible to run schools in Afghanistan unless there are American troops to protect them. But that's incorrect.

CARE, a humanitarian organization, operates 300 schools in Afghanistan, and not one has been burned by the Taliban. Greg Mortenson, of *Three Cups of Tea* fame, has overseen the building of 145 schools in Afghanistan and Pakistan and operates dozens more in tents or rented buildings—and he says that not one has been destroyed by the Taliban either.

US Spending Priorities

The high cost of war relative to the risk of terrorism has some people questioning spending priorities. Over a ten-year period, deaths from cancer were vastly greater than deaths from terrorism, yet the United States has spent far more money waging war in Afghanistan and Iraq as part of the war on terror than was spent on cancer research.

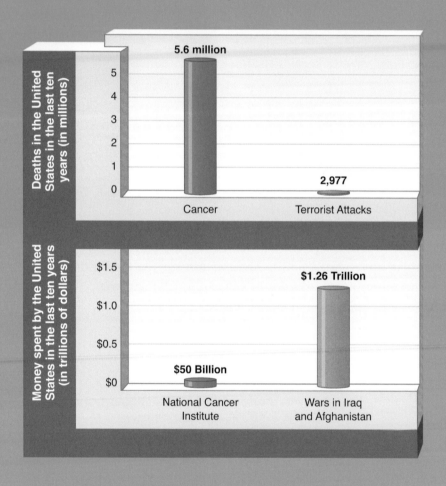

Taken from: Tony Piro. "Ten Years Later." Calamities of Nature, October 7, 2011. www.calamitiesofnature.com /archive/?c=594.

Aid groups show that it is quite possible to run schools so long as there is respectful consultation with tribal elders and buy-in from them. And my hunch is that CARE and Mr. Mortenson are doing more to bring peace to Afghanistan than Mr. Obama's surge of troops.

The American military has been eagerly reading "Three Cups of Tea" but hasn't absorbed the central lesson: building schools is a better bet for peace than firing missiles (especially when one cruise missile costs about as much as building 11 schools).

Mr. Mortenson lamented to me that for the cost of just 246 soldiers posted for one year, America could pay for a higher education plan for all Afghanistan. That would help build an Afghan economy, civil society and future—all for one-quarter of 1 percent of our military spending in Afghanistan this year.

The latest uproar over Pakistani hand-holding with the Afghan Taliban underscores that billions of dollars in U.S. military aid just doesn't buy the loyalty it used to. In contrast, education can actually transform a nation. That's one reason Bangladesh is calmer than Pakistan, Oman is less threatening than Yemen.

Paradoxically, the most eloquent advocate in government for balance in financing priorities has been Mr. Gates, the defense secretary. He has noted that the military has more people in its marching bands than the State Department has diplomats.

Faced with constant demands for more, Mr. Gates in May [2010] asked: "Is it a dire threat that by 2020 the United States will have only 20 times more advanced stealth fighters than China?"

In the presidential campaign, Mr. Obama promised to invest in a global education fund. Since then, he seems to have forgotten the idea—even though he is spending enough every five weeks in Afghanistan to ensure that practically every child on our planet gets a primary education.

We won our nation's independence for $2.4 billion in today's money, the Congressional Research Service report said. That was good value, considering that we now fritter the same amount every nine days in Afghanistan. Mr. Obama, isn't it time to rebalance our priorities?

SEVEN

The United States Needs to Accept and Work with Afghan Corruption

George H. Wittman

> George H. Wittman writes a weekly column on inter-
> national affairs for the *American Spectator* and was the
> founding chairman of the National Institute for Public
> Policy. In the following viewpoint Wittman argues that
> the United States must work with Afghanistan's estab-
> lished system of bribery in order to achieve its goals there.
> According to the author, many places operate through a
> similar system of paying off various people in order to get
> things done, including the United States itself. Wittman
> says that some of those involved in Afghan corruption
> are accomplishing much that is in the interests of the
> United States. In order to operate effectively, he suggests,
> the United States and NATO (North Atlantic Treaty
> Organization) must accept and intelligently work with the
> corrupt power structure that exists in the country.

The issue of corruption becomes ever more complicated when a developing country is fighting for its existence—militarily, politically, economically—and the national leadership must work its hardest to provide advantages to politically strong elements who are loyal to the central government. This is only logical; it's been the logic of the American presence in Afghanistan from the very beginning.

Why then is Washington so upset with the so-called corrupt government of [Afghan president] Hamid Karzai? Did he not dispense largesse to those friendly factions that supported him? Did he not use some of the U.S. aid to buy off some of the more moderate Taliban leadership? Did he not ensure that his brother (who has been charged by the American media as a drug kingpin) use his paramilitary contacts to counter anti-government operations in Kandahar and Helmand?

The author points to the well-organized payoff system of Herat governor Ismail Khan (shown) as an example of Afghan corruption.

The answer of course is that President Hamid Karzai did all that—and more. And he did it with the full knowledge of the American political apparatus in Kabul [capital of Afghanistan] and Washington. Perhaps the American officials did not know the full details. And perhaps they didn't know the exact amounts that slipped into the Karzai family's private accounts. But the Americans didn't want to know. That's called the "old Chicago" way. It's also not unknown in Texas.

Culturally Approved Bribery

Apparently one of the things that upset Washington most was to find out that the construction monies of AID [Agency for International Development] were finding their way into the hands of certain Afghan businessmen in the construction trade who were known to be friendly with the Taliban. Old timers immediately remembered Vietnam, and older timers remembered the days of the Korean War and the corrupt but U.S.-favored leadership of Syngman Rhee. It's a story as ancient as history itself, and certainly not limited to the American experience.

Fifty years ago the late Kenneth Dadzie, who went on to be Secretary General of UNCTAD (United Nations Conference on Trade and Development), explained away the existence of graft in newly independent countries as follows: "Yes, there is at least fifteen per cent placed on the top of every government contract that is for the political leadership to do with what they wish. That money goes mostly to the tribal and union leaders who are the ones who carry the burden of the local scene. I wish it was otherwise, but that is the reality of the moment. I assure you it's all well organized. If this 'dash' system wasn't well organized—well, that would be criminal."

One of the best examples of this culturally approved, well-organized system of "payoff" is found in the region of northwestern Afghanistan around Herat. This region has been dominated for many years by Ismail Khan, a former Afghan Army officer, who had fought against the Soviets and subsequently the Taliban. Khan, when he was governor of the province, built

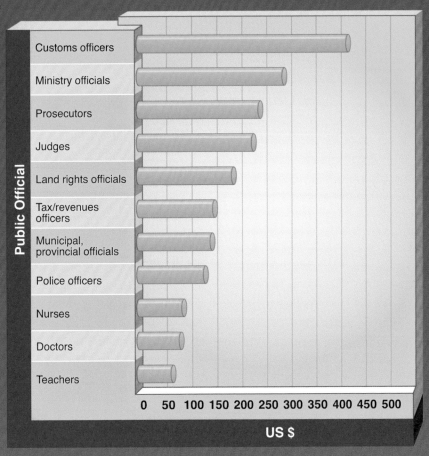

Average Value of Bribes Paid to Public Officials in Afghanistan

Public Official (vertical axis)

- Customs officers
- Ministry officials
- Prosecutors
- Judges
- Land rights officials
- Tax/revenues officers
- Municipal, provincial officials
- Police officers
- Nurses
- Doctors
- Teachers

0 50 100 150 200 250 300 350 400 450 500

US $

Taken from: BBC News. "UN Afghanistan Survey Points to Huge Scale of Bribery," January 19, 2010. http://news.bbc .co.uk/2/hi/8466915.stm.

his political base by husbanding taxes that had been collected and using them for local development rather than shifting a portion of the revenue to Kabul that Afghan government regulations require. His well-equipped private army has kept the Herat region secure in the face of repeated Taliban efforts to destabilize the province.

Working with the Existing System

Khan remains a key figure in the new Karzai cabinet and is an essential component in the struggle against the Taliban. Reality therefore dictates that Ismail Khan and his Herat followers must be favored to continue their efforts to maintain a strong front against Taliban efforts and interests. This takes money and resources. Is it corrupt to especially reward Khan and others like him in order to build and preserve a pro-Western Afghan rule? Was Ken Dadzie wrong? More to the point, would Washington reorder its own standing domestic political methodology?

The Afghan nation is made up of many individuals in leadership posts—tribal, political, military—all of whom carry claims on the central government. They may not have as broad-ranging influence as the man from Herat, but each in their own way is important to creating and maintaining stability toward the objective of countering Taliban influence.

If the U.S. and NATO [North Atlantic Treaty Organization] intend to be effective in Afghanistan, they will have to understand and deal with the phenomenon of Afghan tribal orientation and dominance. It's a bit like operating in Chicago or elsewhere in the United States where established political power dominates. You have to know where the levers are, and then you have to know when, where, and how to pull them.

EIGHT

The War Is Not Helping the Rights of Women in Afghanistan

Johnny Barber

Johnny Barber has visited Afghanistan as a member of a delegation from Voices for Creative Non-Violence. He has also traveled to Iraq, Israel, Palestine, Lebanon, Jordan, and Syria to bear witness and document the suffering of people who are affected by war. In the following viewpoint Barber argues that women and children are worse off since the United States and allied countries invaded Afghanistan in 2001. According to the author, women continue to be considered property in Afghanistan, and the US-supported government led by Hamid Karzai has passed laws banning women from leaving their homes without permission from their husbands. He says the continuing widespread practice of women's committing suicide by setting themselves on fire is a sign of how bad things are for women there. Barber claims that the occupation of Afghanistan, far from improving the lives of women and children there, is actually part of the problem.

In Kabul, [the capital of Afghanistan,] the children are everywhere. You see them scrounging through trash. You see them doing manual labor in the auto body shops, the butchers, and the construction sites. They carry teapots and glasses from shop to shop. You see them moving through the snarled traffic swirling small pots of pungent incense, warding off evil spirits and trying to collect small change. They can be found sleeping in doorways or in the rubble of destroyed buildings. It is estimated that 70,000 children live on the streets of Kabul.

The big news story on CNN [Cable News Network] this morning [Oct. 17, 2011,] is the excitement generated as hundreds of people line up to buy the newest iPhone. I can't stop thinking of the children sitting in the dirt of the refugee camp, or running down the path pushing old bicycle tires, or the young boy sitting next to his overflowing sacks of collected detritus [trash]. He has a deep infection on the corner of his mouth that looks terribly infected. These images contrast with an image of an old grandfather, dressed in a spotless all white shalwar kameez squatting on the sidewalk outside a huge iron gate, embracing his beautiful young grand daughter in a huge hug, each smiling broadly, one of the few moments of joy I have witnessed on the streets of Kabul.

Worse Off Since the Invasion

In Afghanistan, one in five children die before their 5th birthday, (41% of the deaths occur in the first month of life). For the children who make it past the first month, many perish due to preventable and highly treatable conditions including diarrhea and pneumonia. Malnourishment affects 39% of the children, compared to 25% at the start of the U.S. invasion; 52% don't have access to clean water; 94% of births are not registered. The children are afforded very little legal protection, especially girls, who are [still] banned from schools in many regions, used as collateral to settle debts, and married through arranged marriages [at] as young as 10 years old. Though not currently an issue, HIV/AIDS looms as a catastrophic possibility as drug addiction increases significantly, even among women and children. Only 16% of women use modern contraception, and children on the streets are vulnerable to sexual exploitation. This is why the "State of the World's Mothers" report issued in May 2011 by Save the Children ranked Afghanistan last, with only Somalia providing worse outcomes for their children.

Retired Army Col. John Agoglia said, "A key to America's long-term national security and one of the best ways for our nation to make friends around the world is by promoting the health of women and children in fragile and emerging nations"—in Afghanistan, this strategy is failing. Not a single public hospital has been built since the invasion. It is not an impossibility; it is a matter of will. Emergency, an Italian NGO [nongovernmental organization], runs 3 hospitals and 30 clinics throughout Afghanistan on a budget of 7 million dollars per year. This is ISAF's NATO's [North Atlantic Treaty Organization's] International Security Assistance Force) monthly budget for air-conditioning.

Polls have consistently shown that over 90 percent of Americans believe saving children should be a national priority. Children comprise 65% of the Afghan population. Afghanistan was named the worst place on earth to be a child. In Afghanistan children have been sacrificed by the United States, collateral damage in our "war on terror."

Women Are Considered Property

The mothers of these at risk children are not faring any better. Most are illiterate. Most are chronically malnourished; 1 woman in 11 dies in pregnancy or childbirth, this compares to 1 in 2,100 in the US (the highest of any industrialized nation). In Italy and Ireland, the risk of maternal death is less than 1 in 15,000 and in Greece it's 1 in 31,800. Skilled health professionals attend only 14% of childbirths. A woman's life expectancy is barely 45 years of age.

Women are still viewed as property. A law has been passed by the Karzai regime that legalizes marital rape, and requires a woman to get the permission of her husband to leave the house. Domestic violence is a chronic problem. A woman who runs away from home (even if escaping violence) is imprisoned. Upon completion of her sentence she is returned to the husband. Self-immolation [committing suicide by setting oneself on fire] is still common as desperate women try to get out of impossible situations.

Shortly after the U.S. invasion, [First Lady] Laura Bush said, "The plight of women and children in Afghanistan is a matter of deliberate human cruelty, carried out by those who seek to

Afghan girls have very little legal protection. They are banned from attending school in many regions, used as debt collateral that is akin to slavery, and forced into marriages at as young as ten years old.

intimidate and control." President [George W.] Bush said, "Our coalition has liberated Afghanistan and restored fundamental human rights and freedoms to Afghan women, and all the people of Afghanistan." Actually, the former warlords responsible for the destruction, pillage, and rape of Afghanistan were ushered back into power by the United States. In 2007, these very same warlords, now Parliamentarians, passed a bill that granted amnesty for any killings during the civil war. A local journalist said, "The killers are the ones holding the pens, writing the law and continuing their crimes."

The Worst Security Situation in Years

When [Afghan women's rights activist] Malalai Joya addressed the Peace Loya Jirga [a "grand assembly" to discuss matters of national significance] convened in December, 2003, she boldly asked, "Why are we allowing criminals to be present here?" She was thrown out of the assembly. Undeterred, she ran for Parliament, winning in a landslide. She began her maiden speech in Parliament by saying, "My condolences to the people of Afghanistan. . . ." As she continued speaking, the warlord sitting behind her threatened to rape and kill her. The MP's [members of Parliament] voted her out of Parliament and Karzai upheld her ouster. In hiding, she continues to champion women's rights. She has stated that the only people who can liberate Afghan women are the women themselves. When we spoke briefly to her by phone, she stated that she was surprised to still be alive, and needed to cancel our meeting, as it was too dangerous in the current [2011] security situation. The Red Cross states that the security situation is the worst it has been in 30 years.

In America, as our total defense budget balloons to 667 billion dollars per year, women and children are faring worse as well. In the "State of the World's Mothers" report, America has dropped from 11th in 2003 to 31st of the developed countries today. We currently rank behind such luminaries as Estonia, Croatia, and Slovakia. We fall even farther in regards to our children, going from the 4th ranked country to the 34th. Poverty is on the increase with an estimated 1 child in 5 living in poverty. More than 20 million children rely on school lunch programs to keep from going hungry. The number of people living in poverty in America has grown by 2.6 million in just the last 12 months.

Dear reader, I hesitate to bother you with so many statistics, I eliminated the pie charts and graphs, and this report is still dull. After all, the new iPhone has Siri, a personal assistant that understands you when you speak. You can verbally instruct it to send a text message, and it does! Now that's excitement! CNN states there is no need to panic; the Atlanta store has plenty of phones to fill the demand.

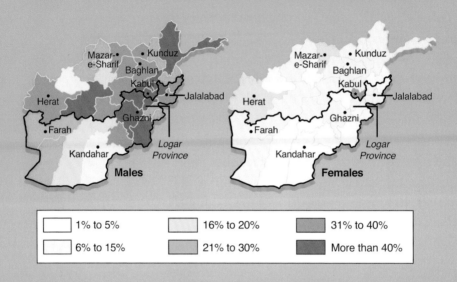

Literacy Rates in Afghanistan, by Province

Males

Females

1% to 5%	16% to 20%	31% to 40%
6% to 15%	21% to 30%	More than 40%

Taken from: Yaroslav Trofimov. "Emboldened Taliban Try to Sell Softer Image." *Wall Street Journal*, January 28, 2012. http://online.wsj.com/article/SB10001424052970203806504577177074111336352.html.

Failing to Protect Women and Children

Looking only at numbers it is easy to avoid the truth of the enormous amount of human suffering they envelop. Drive through the streets of any American city and these statistics come alive in the swollen ranks of the homeless. Drive through the streets of Kabul and these statistics come alive in the forms of hungry children begging for change.

It is difficult to ascertain what benefit America is deriving from our continued military presence in Afghanistan, though exploitation of natural resources certainly plays a role. Hundreds of billions of dollars are being spent in a military strategy that is failing by all indicators. Yet the politicians in this country continue to back this strategy. Arms dealers and contractors, like G.E. [General Electric] and Boeing, all with lobbyists on Capitol Hill, continue to reap big financial rewards and in turn reward politicians with financial support. Our politicians claim to be "tough on terror" and profess we are "winning." But by what measure do they ascertain this? The only Afghan people benefiting from our presence are the people supporting the occupation forces, the warlords, and the drug lords. As the poppy fields produce record yields, "poppy palaces" are springing up all over Kabul, ostentatious signs that someone is benefiting from our interference.

One measure to judge the success of a nation is its ability to protect its most vulnerable populations. America is not succeeding. The plight of women and children in Afghanistan is still a matter of deliberate human cruelty, carried out by those who seek to intimidate and control. When will our politicians hear the desperate cry of the street children of Afghanistan, who, with all the incense in the world, simply can't ward off the evil of our occupation?

NINE

Use of Children as Suicide Bombers Is a Serious Problem in the War in Afghanistan

Thomas Bell

Thomas Bell is a journalist in Kathmandu, Nepal. In the following viewpoint Bell argues that the war in Afghanistan has seen an increasing use of children as suicide bombers, often recruited (or kidnapped) and trained in Pakistan and then smuggled across the border into Afghanistan or sometimes used for attacks in Pakistan itself. The author claims that children are more easily turned into suicide bombers because they are more impressionable than adults and do not have a fully developed sense of their own mortality. He says the Taliban teach them that the United States is the enemy of Islam and that anyone who allies themselves with the United States (including the Pakistan army and government) is a legitimate target of bombing—even regular Muslims if they are not actively fighting against the United States. According to the author, many of the child bombers have been recruited during the war in the tribal areas of Pakistan that border Afghanistan (an area which is not fully controlled by the Pakistan government and in which many Taliban from Afghanistan are operating). However, he says there is increasing evidence that recruitment is also spreading to other, more settled areas of Pakistan.

The video cannot quite avoid the impression of a childish game. The boy selected for the martyrdom operation, dressed in black, walks down a line of his young friends, embracing each one for the last time. The camera seems to be held at adult-height. It follows the bomber as he walks towards his target—another group of children. One of them tries to stop him, but he evades the security. A plume of dust is thrown up in the air in an uncanny simulation of an explosion. The bomber and his targets lie on the ground, pretending to be dead, trying to keep the smiles off their faces.

When this video popped up on the Internet earlier this year, many in Pakistan were deeply disturbed by the story it told of how children have become psychologically and physically involved in the violence in the country. According to Salma Jafar of Save the Children UK [United Kingdom] in Pakistan, 'It's horrifying and alarming. These children have become fascinated by bombers rather than condemning them. If they glamorise violence now, they can become part of it later in life.'

In both Pakistan and Afghanistan, hundreds of children have been among the civilian victims of ground fighting and air strikes. Suicide bombings were introduced to the war in Afghanistan in 2003 (during that year there were two such attacks), and became increasingly common after 2005. The tactic spread from there to Pakistan. During the Islamabad Red Mosque siege in 2007, mothers sympathetic to militancy dressed their children in suicide-bomber costumes, with fake bomb vests. An increasing number of children have been made to wear the real thing.

Recruited in Pakistan

As many as 90 percent of suicide bombers in Pakistan are 12 to 18, according to editor and author Zahid Hussain. In July, a child bomber as young as nine was arrested while trying to cross from Pakistan to Afghanistan. Analysts say that a string of individual cases show that some of the child suicide bombers used in Afghanistan are recruited and trained in Pakistan before being sent—or sold—to be used in attacks across the border. The price of a child bomber, reportedly between USD [US$] 7000 and USD 14,000, depends on how close to the target they are expected to get.

Children are easier to indoctrinate or coerce. The 'youth bulge' in Pakistan's population (60 percent of Pakistanis are under 25), and the poor condition of state education in the country, offers the Taliban a practically inexhaustible pool of vulnerable boys to be turned into live ammunition. The would-be bombers being rehabilitated at the Sabawoon school, in Malakand [Pakistan] . . . epitomise the typical profile of these children. According to Muhammad Farooq Khan, who taught at the school, they often come from large and extremely poor families in remote rural areas. (Khan was murdered in October last year [2010]. Unsurprisingly, many people working to rehabilitate indoctrinated children prefer to remain anonymous.) They lack positive male role models. Before they are lured away by extremists, most have had no experience of life outside their villages.

Most at the school were educated not at madrassas [Islamic religious schools] but at government schools. Despite widespread assumptions, several studies have shown that madrassa education is not the common path into militancy. Partly that is because madrassas account for but a small proportion of Pakistan's schools. Meanwhile, the government sector often turns out barely educated children ill equipped to resist indoctrination.

"Goats for Sacrifice"

In the training camp, the children's family ties are severed. They place their trust in alternative or surrogate sources of guidance and authority. Accounts of the indoctrination process agree that trainee bombers are systematically cut off from alternative sources of information. Religious teachings emphasise violent jihad and martyrdom.

The common term used by extremist clerics for these children is *qurbani ka bakra*, or 'goats for sacrifice,' 'Children are tools to achieve god's will, and whatever comes your way, you sacrifice it,' says to Qari Hussain, a former Taliban commander notori-

Two Afghan boys accused of being suicide bombers are led to their cells at the Kabul Juvenile Rehabilitation Center. Many child suicide bombers are recruited by religious leaders in remote areas of Afghanistan and Pakistan.

ous for training bombers. Hussain is reported to have died in an American drone strike that killed around 80 people at a funeral in South Waziristan [Pakistan] earlier this year [2011].

In 2010 the Pakistan Army captured a facility, painted with scenes of paradise, where children were trained for suicide bombing. In contrast to the barren mountains all around, heaven was depicted with green hills and rivers of milk and honey. The virgins who are said to await martyrs lined the river banks. While adult bombers might experience some 'existential grappling' at the idea of their own death, if not at that of others, children might not be able to fully comprehend the end of their own lives, especially when the afterlife is presented as so close at hand.

"No One Is Innocent"

Psychologists describe how children are malleable and impressionable; a person's awareness of mortality and moral sense is absorbed during childhood. The trainers show them videos of purported atrocities against Muslims. They are offered a simple polarising narrative in which the US is both the enemy of Islam and an ally of the Pakistani state; likewise, the Pakistan Army is so tainted by association with the 'infidel' that it is scarcely seen as Muslim at all. Captured would-be bombers parrot the same line when they are asked about the ordinary Muslims who would be among their victims: Unless they are fighting against the enemies of Islam, 'no one is innocent.'

What we see here is a 180-degree inversion of moral norms. 'No matter who, no matter why, no one, at any point, has the right to use children as instruments of war and destruction. It is the most extreme form of abuse and an act of twisted cowardice to turn a child into a bomb,' says Sarah Crowe, spokesperson for UNICEF [United Nations International Children's Emergency Fund] South Asia. 'Children are the very essence of humanity—using them as military tools brutalises humanity and criminalises their childhood. They have no place in any form in any conflict and it is the duty of all to do their utmost to protect children from acts of violence.'

Scholars of militancy point out that suicide attacks typically cause higher casualties and are therefore attractive for relatively weak contenders in asymmetric conflicts. They also prove not so much the fanatical determination of the perpetrators as their willingness to exploit others for their purpose. Suicide attacks generate more anxiety and a sense of helplessness, fear and disturbance in society compared to other methods—the more so if the bomber is a child or a woman. These effects help to generate intense media coverage. But some necessary conditions must be present before a suicide strategy will work. The perpetrator's passive supporters in the wider population must be sufficiently polarised against the enemy that they are willing to support, or excuse, the tactic. Among the group's active members, the radicalisation process must be so extreme that they are willing to participate, or to groom children, to carry out suicide attacks.

Sexual Abuse of Child-Bombers

It is interesting, then, that while Afghanistan's National Directorate of Security claimed in June [2011] to be holding 100 would-be suicide bombers between the ages of 12 and 17, local militants denied the claim. 'It's our policy not to recruit children—in order to prevent vice in our ranks because most mujahideen [Islamic guerilla fighters] are single men and spend a lot of their time away from their homes, so the policy is to avoid any child sexual abuse in our forces,' a Taliban spokesperson was quoted as saying. In fact, accounts from captured child-bombers in Pakistan suggest that sexual abuse does sometimes occur in training camps.

Recent evidence from Afghanistan indicates that patterns of recruitment might be shifting. Lotfullah Mashal, spokesperson for the National Directorate of Security, told the UK *Daily Telegraph* in May [2011] that four young bombers recently captured at the border were all from the Pakistani city of Attock. 'In the past we have had suicide attackers from Waziristan and Bajaur,' Mashal said, 'but this is the first time we have arrested child suicide attackers from the settled [nontribal] areas of Pakistan.'

Two recent cases in Pakistan also suggest that patterns could be changing. In June [2011], two men in Karachi [Pakistan] confessed to kidnapping children and selling them for terrorist training in Waziristan. In the same month, a nine-year-old girl was snatched on her way to school in Peshawar [Pakistan]. A few days later her kidnappers changed her private-school uniform for a state-school one, strapped her with eight kilograms of explosives, and told her to push the button when she reached a police checkpost. The girl seemed to understand enough to raise an alarm, and the bomb was safely defused.

TEN

The Teenage Son of a Soldier in Afghanistan Describes the Impact of His Father's Military Service

Chad, as told to Deborah Ellis

> Chad is a seventeen-year-old Canadian boy whose father is one of the coalition soldiers fighting alongside US forces in Afghanistan. In the following viewpoint he describes how his father changed after serving for six months in the Afghanistan war, with negative consequences for his parents' marriage and their family life.

*T*he stress soldiers experience doesn't end when they leave the war zone. Sometimes being back at home and away from military surroundings is when the stress begins to catch up to them. Family members can find themselves living with a very different person from the one they knew.

This condition, sometimes called battle fatigue, post-traumatic stress disorder or operational stress injury, takes many forms. Some soldiers experience nightmares, depression, sensitivity to loud noises, and feelings of being out of place. Some experience the sensations of war in odd moments at home, triggered by a sound or a scent. Others find it difficult to be close to people in the same way they were before they went overseas.

Being in a war zone—seeing and being with people who are suffering, being in a place where danger is all around—is bound to affect the people who go through it. Some parents, after spending months around children who are hungry and have no schooling, lose patience when their own children carry on like regular North American kids, wanting this and that and complaining about homework. Others return home changed in a positive way, more appreciative of their families and less likely to get angry at small things.

Since there is no standard way that parents behave when they come home from war, it's hard for kids to know what to expect.

Chad's father is with the Canadian military at CFB [Canadian forces base] Trenton. He recently returned from a tour in Kandahar, Afghanistan.

Returning from Afghanistan

My father is serving with the military. He's trying to make chief. There are 210 people under him directly. He maintains aircraft. He started out with the military police, then he moved into maintenance. I have an older brother who is twenty-three, and an older sister who is eighteen. My mother works as a dispatcher.

My father just got back from Kandahar, where he was building roads and a police station. He's been overseas a lot. He was in Africa a couple of times, and Dubai [United Arab Emirates]. He's on alert status more than half the time, so he's been away a lot. Kandahar was pretty dangerous. There was a lot of stuff going through the line, rockets and things, and he had a couple of bomb threats as well.

That's kind of been his life. There was one time he was in Rwanda, going down the street, and they had to stop and when he looked over there was a little kid who had an M16 to his head. He was in Rwanda just after the massacres [in 1994]. He saw all the bodies and the body parts strewn around. He's still going through the treatment to get over what he saw. I was around eight at the time.

After he got back from Rwanda there were certain sounds or smells that made him snap. Before, he was just nice and quiet and easy. I'm not quite sure which sounds or smells set him off, but my mom always talks about it.

He was in Rwanda just once, for six or eight months. Like I said, he's still in treatment for that, and the military keeps sending him overseas.

Things Changed After Afghanistan

As soon as my father got back from Kandahar, my parents decided to split. It was his decision, really. He told us that as soon as he set foot on the Canadian tarmac, he stopped knowing what he wanted, so they split. He got back on March 1 [2008], and as soon as he stepped off the plane and hit the landing strip, he decided he didn't know what he wanted.

My mother had no clue about any of this while he was away. None of us did. They emailed each other all the time, and everything seemed normal, but as soon as he got back and stepped on Canadian soil, he was just—he went blank, and he I didn't know what he wanted.

That was a couple of months ago. I haven't asked him for an explanation. We don't talk about anything.

My mother was so surprised. They'd been married for twenty-three years, and she had no idea this is what was coming. She said that when he got back from Afghanistan he was acting a lot different. He was trying to control stuff. It was weird, the things that were happening in the house. It was different from before. I didn't notice so much because I just go to school and then to work, so I wasn't home much.

Distracted and Absent

Dad was in Kandahar for six months. I emailed him there. We talked about how we were going to go fishing when he got back, maybe get a car and fix it up for the drag races. We were talking about how he was going to retire, but that's not happening now.

An American serviceman is greeted by his family upon his return from a tour of duty in Afghanistan. Many returning vets face post-traumatic stress disorder and feel alienated from their families.

He's staying in for a few more years. He wants to get his chief ranking.

Before Kandahar, he was quiet, but he always wanted to do stuff with us. Now he's always running around all over the place, trying to keep himself busy.

He lives on the base with me. We moved my mom down to Kingston [Ontario, Canada,] last Saturday and my dad and I live here on the base so I can finish high school here. We share a house, and we hang out, but we don't talk.

No Talk About Kandahar

I'm used to waking up and having my mom here, so it's different for me. Now it's just him, and he's not really here. I'm glad I can talk about this with my brother. He's a police officer in Kingston.

I wish I knew what happened to Dad in Kandahar. He won't talk about it. I think he's afraid he'll end up scaring us because of what he went through. It makes me lonely, but I don't worry about stuff he doesn't want to talk about. I'll let him come to me if he wants to, but I don't think he'll want to. His temper is short, but it's always been short.

I do know that there was an American civilian killed by a suicide bomber just a few yards away from my dad. That would change anybody.

I've got lots of friends, not just kids from the base. Most of my friends live in the city, and we drive around, go to parties, whatever.

Hopefully I'll go into the police college and become a cop like my brother. I wouldn't want to join the army because I wouldn't want to be away from my family. I couldn't do that.

I think my relationship with my dad will still be steady. Hopefully we'll still have our fishing trips, like old times. That would be good. Mom's doing okay, although she's still kind of in shock.

I honestly don't know what Canada is doing in Afghanistan. I just tried to keep my mom nice and cool when Dad was over there. Even though things are different now, as long as my dad is home safe, I'm happy.

What You Should Know About the War in Afghanistan

Facts About the War in Afghanistan

The Brookings Institution, in its report *Afghanistan Index*, reported on March 31, 2012:

- In November 2001, a month after the war began, there were 1,300 US troops in Afghanistan.
- In September 2011, in addition to 98,000 US soldiers, there were 40,670 other foreign troops; total troops and security forces (including Afghan forces) equaled 445,573.
- In 2007 there were 38,000 private Defense Department contractors working in Afghanistan; by March 2011 that number had increased to 90,000.
- In September 2007 there were less than 4,000 private security contractors in Afghanistan; by March 2011 there were over 18,000.

According to the US Department of Defense, in its *Report on Progress Toward Security and Stability in Afghanistan*, published in April 2012:

- On September 30, 2011, there were about 97,795 US troops in Afghanistan; by March 31, 2012, that number had fallen to 86,692.
- Between March 2011 and March 31, 2012, Afghan National Security Forces (ANSF) had grown from 284,952 personnel to 344,108; this includes 149,642 police and 194,466 soldiers.

- As of March 2012 the ANSF has assumed responsibility for the security of nearly half of the population of Afghanistan.
- Following five years of sharply increasing EIA (enemy-initiated attacks), the rate of attacks fell by 9 percent from 2010 to 2011 and saw a further 16 percent reduction by April 2012.
- There was a 30 percent reduction in complex and coordinated attacks from October 2011 to March 2012 compared with the previous year.
- By March 31, 2012, via the Afghanistan Peace and Reintegration Program (APRP) initiated in July 2010 by President Karzai, 3,907 insurgents had been taken from the battlefield and enrolled in the peace process.

According to the ISAF [International Security Assistance Force] report *Monthly Data: Trends Through February 2012:*

- IED (improvised explosive device) and mine attacks were 32 percent lower in February 2012 than in February 2011.
- In February 2012 over half of the IEDs and mines planted by insurgents were discovered and defused before they exploded.
- Civilian casualties caused by the ISAF were down 77 percent in January and February 2012, compared with the same two months the previous year.
- In February 2010 more than 90 percent of civilian casualties were caused by insurgents, rather than the US and allied forces.

According to Jeffrey Bordin's report *A Crisis of Trust and Cultural Incompatibility*, published on May 12, 2011:

- At least twenty-six cases of murder or attempted murder of ISAF/UNAMA (International Security Assistance Force/ United Nations Assistance Mission in Afghanistan) personnel were committed by ANSF or ASG (Afghan Security Guard) forces since May 2007.
- On average, one UNAMA or ISAF member was killed by an ASG or ANSF member every twelve days during the twenty months preceding May 2011.

- Such cases happened at an increasing pace in the six-month period preceding May 2011: An average of one ISAF member was murdered by ANSF/ASG forces every six days during that period.
- Between November 29, 2010, and May 12, 2011, 16 percent of all ISAF deaths resulting from hostile action were the result of murders committed by ASG/ANSF forces.

The Brookings Institution's *Afghanistan Index* reported the following on March 31, 2012:

- In 2009 there was more than one assassination per month on average in and around Kandahar.
- In 2010 assassinations in and around Kandahar had increased to more than five per month.
- In 2011 the number climbed to over ten per month.
- In 2004 there were an estimated 1,700–3,200 insurgency soldiers fighting in Afghanistan; by 2010, there were over 30,000.

According to an article in the *Georgetown Journal of International Affairs* published on April 24, 2012:

- By October 2012 the war in Afghanistan will have lasted 11 years; in comparison, the American Civil War lasted 4 years, US involvement in World War II lasted 3.5 years, and "significant American involvement" in Vietnam lasted about 8.5 years.

Cost and Consequences of the War in Afghanistan

The Brookings *Afghanistan Index* reported the following on March 31, 2012:

- Between the start of the war on October 7, 2001, and March 31, 2012, 1,917 US troops had been killed and 1,017 non-US coalition troops had been killed, for a total of 2,934 coalition troop deaths.

- Between October 30, 2001, and March 31, 2012, 15,516 US troops had been wounded in action.
- As of February 29, 2012, the highest losses among non-US coalition troops, by country, were 398 British fatalities, 158 Canadian fatalities, and 82 French fatalities.
- Between October 30, 2001, and March 31, 2012, 1,095 private contractors died.
- From January 2007 through 2011, 1,561 Afghan National Army (ANA) personnel and 4,120 Afghan National Police (ANP) personnel died.
- In 2005, 6 percent of US soldiers indicated that they were experiencing acute stress; this figure rose to 13.2 percent in 2009, and further increased to 17.4 percent in 2010.
- From fiscal year (FY) 2001 through the budget request for FY 2012, total funding for the war in Afghanistan equaled $523.5 billion for the Department of Defense, $29.4 billion for State Department/US AID (United States Agency for International Development), and $4.2 billion for the US Department of Veterans Affairs medical services.

ProPublica, in its in-depth report *Brain Wars: How the Military Is Failing Its Wounded*, published in 2011–2012, states:

- Approximately 20 percent of soldiers received a concussion (a mild traumatic brain injury) while serving in Afghanistan.
- Most soldiers who sustain concussions recover in less than two weeks; however, an estimated 5–15 percent suffer ongoing cognitive difficulties.
- 7.5 percent of combat soldiers who served in Afghanistan exhibited at least three symptoms of post-concussion syndrome (a complex disorder occurring after a concussion that persists for some time); an additional 20 percent had one symptom.
- In 2010 between 48 and 56 percent of soldiers in Afghanistan said they were "directly responsible" for killing an enemy soldier; around the time levels of violence peaked in Iraq (in 2006), only 12–15 percent of soldiers there said they had killed an enemy soldier.

According to a *Los Angeles Times* article published on April 7, 2012:

- Almost 8 percent of soldiers on active duty are using sedatives;
- Over 6 percent of soldiers on active duty are taking antidepressants, an eightfold increase since 2005;
- In 2011 over 110,000 US soldiers on active duty were using prescribed sedatives, narcotics, antidepressants, antianxiety drugs, or antipsychotic medication.

James Kitfield, in his *National Journal* article "The Longest Deployment," published on July 23, 2010, reported that

- in 2001 the suicide rate among US soldiers was 9.1 per 100,000; by 2009 the rate had increased by 71 percent to 15.6 per 100,000.

ABC News reported on May 1, 2012, that

- between 2007 (when the United Nations started reporting statistics on civilian casualties) and 2011, 11,864 civilians had been killed in the war.

Amnesty International's report *Fleeing War, Finding Misery: The Plight of the Internally Displaced in Afghanistan*, released in 2012, states:

- In 2010 civilian deaths were 25 percent higher than in 2009, increasing by a further 8 percent in 2011.
- Child casualties increased by 21 percent from 2009 to 2010.
- More than 3,000 Afghan civilians died in 2011 due to the war.
- Air strikes by coalition forces caused 9 percent more deaths in 2011 compared with the previous year and included at least 11 children working on farms.
- From 2006 to 2010 an average of 400 people experienced internal displacement (forced to flee their homes and move somewhere else in the country) every day, one-third of which were children under 18.

- Each year since 2008 the number of displaced people in Afghanistan has increased.
- Between January and June 2010, 42,000 people were internally displaced; in the same six-month period of 2011, 91,000 were displaced, an increase of 46 percent.
- About 25 percent of the 433,000 internally displaced people in Afghanistan (as of March 2011) had been displaced since at least 2002.
- In January 2012 an estimated 500,000 Afghans in total were internally displaced.
- As of 2012, 2.8 million Afghan refugees lived outside the country.

Signs of Progress for the People of Afghanistan

The Brookings Institution, in its publication *Afghanistan Index*, reported on March 31, 2012:

- In 2002 electricity capacity in Afghanistan was only 243 Mw (megawatts); by 2009 it was 1028.5 Mw.
- In 2002 there were an estimated 1 million phone users in Afghanistan; in 2010, there were 12 million.
- In 2001, before the war began, it is estimated that less than 1 million students were enrolled in elementary or secondary school; by 2011, 8 million children were enrolled.
- Life expectancy for men in Afghanistan was 42 in 2004, rising to 62 in 2010.
- Life expectancy for women in Afghanistan was 42 in 2004, rising to 64 in 2010.
- The mortality rate (per 1,000 live births) for infants in Afghanistan was 165 in 2003, dropping to 77 in 2010.
- The mortality rate for children under 5 was 257 in 2003, dropping to 97 in 2010.

According to the US Department of Defense in its *Report on Progress Toward Security and Stability in Afghanistan*, released in April 2012:

- The GDP (gross domestic product) of Afghanistan grew by 8 percent in 2010 and 7 percent in 2011.

- In 2002 there were 498 health facilities in Afghanistan, increasing to 2,136 by April 2012.
- The rate of women dying in childbirth dropped from 1,600 to 327 for every 100,000 births between 2002 and 2010.
- Only 9 percent of the population in 2002 could get to basic health services within a two-hour walk; in 2012, 68 percent of the population could access health services within a one-hour walk.
- As of 2012 over 13,000 schools were open in Afghanistan, staffed by over 170,000 teachers.
- By 2015 it is estimated that 77 percent of youth in Afghanistan will have access to a basic education.

According to the OXFAM International joint briefing paper *High Stakes: Girls' Education in Afghanistan*, released on February 24, 2011:

- Under Taliban rule (preceding the war in 2001) most girls' schools were closed, and enrollment of girls dropped from 32 to 6.4 percent;
- Enrollment of girls increased from about 5,000 under Taliban rule to 2.4 million enrolled in 2011;
- Of girls polled, 71.8 percent would like to continue their schooling, and 64.1 percent would like to finish university;
- Studies indicate that infant mortality falls by 5–10 percent for each year that girls remain in school (Afghanistan has one of the highest rates of infant mortality on earth);
- 1.9 million girls are registered in primary school (grades 1–6);
- 416,854 girls are registered as students in secondary school (grades 7–9);
- 122,480 girls are registered as high school students (grades 10–12);
- The number of women registered at universities has increased by 43.6 percent since 2007;
- Girls 12–16 years old currently have a literacy rate of 37 percent; boys 12–16 have a literacy rate of 62 percent.

Changing US Perceptions

An ABC News/*Washington Post* poll on April 22, 2012, reported that

- 66 percent of Americans believe the war has not been worth fighting—the same rate as opposed the Iraq war in 2007, when opposition to that war reached its highest level;
- only 30 percent support the war in Afghanistan, 3 percentage points lower than the lowest level of support for the Iraq war;
- 60 percent believe most Afghans are opposed to the US mission in Afghanistan, and only 22 percent believe Afghans support the war.

According to a CNN/ORC report in March 2012:

- In 2006, 50 percent of respondents said they were in favor of the war in Afghanistan while 48 percent were opposed;
- On March 24–25, 2012, 25 percent of respondents were in favor of the war while 72 percent were opposed;
- On March 24–25, 2012, 55 percent said they would like all troops to leave before the planned 2014 withdrawal date, 22 percent wanted the United States to stick with the 2014 withdrawal date, and 22 percent wished to see troops remain beyond 2014.
- Asked on March 24–25, 2012, whether the United States was winning the war in Afghanistan 34 percent said winning, and 61 percent said not winning.

According to an Associated Press–GfK poll published on May 8, 2012:

- 48 percent of respondents indicated that US troops in Afghanistan are helping that country transition to stable democracy;

- 36 percent said having US troops in Afghanistan was doing more to hurt the transition to a stable democracy; and
- 14 percent said they did not know whether the presence of US troops was helpful or not.

Changing Opinions in Afghanistan

An ABC News/BBC/ARD poll in November 2010 reported that

- in 2004, 64 percent of Afghans polled indicated that they believed things in Afghanistan were going in the right direction, while 11 percent said things were going in the wrong direction;
- in November 2010, 59 percent believed things were going in the right direction, while 28 percent said they were going in the wrong direction;
- In 2005, 68 percent of Afghans approved of the US role in Afghanistan, while in November 2010, only 32 percent approved;
- in 2005, 74 percent of Afghans had a very unfavorable opinion of the Taliban, while in November 2010, 68 percent held that opinion;
- in 2005, 91 percent of Afghans polled wanted their current government ruling the country, an opinion that dropped to 86 percent in November 2010;
- in 2005 only 1 percent of Afghans said they would rather see the Taliban ruling Afghanistan, rising to 9 percent in November 2010;
- in 2005, 41 percent of respondents felt the Taliban posed the biggest threat to Afghanistan, while 4 percent felt the United States posed the biggest threat;
- in November 2010, 64 percent believed the Taliban posed the biggest threat, while 6 percent felt the United States did.

According to the US Department of Defense's *Report on Progress Toward Security and Stability in Afghanistan*, released in April 2012:

- In September 2011, 85 percent of Afghan citizens responding to polls felt that security in their country was "good" or "fair," rising to 90 percent in a March 2012 poll;
- In September 2011, about 15 percent of Afghans described the security situation as "bad," dropping to about 10 percent in March 2012;
- In March 2012, 73 percent indicated that "the police are capable of protecting their *mantaqa* [area or district]," while 25 percent indicated the police could not do so.

What You Should Do About the War in Afghanistan

Gather Information

The first step in grappling with any complex and controversial issue is to be informed about it. Gather as much information as you can from a variety of sources. The essays in this book form an excellent starting point, representing a variety of viewpoints and approaches to the topic. Your school or local library will be another source of useful information; look there for relevant books, magazines, and encyclopedia entries. The Bibliography and Organizations to Contact sections of this book will give you useful starting points in gathering additional information.

There is a wealth of information and perspectives on the war in Afghanistan in both the US and international media. Internet search engines will be helpful to you in your search. Many blogs and websites have information and articles dealing with the war from a variety of perspectives, including concerned individuals offering their opinions, activist organizations, governmental organizations such as the Department of Defense, and popular media outlets. It may be useful to examine how the war is viewed in other cultures; doing so may give a broader perspective on US attitudes toward the Afghanistan conflict. In addition to US news networks, you might find it useful to look at the perspectives of foreign news outlets such as Al-Jazeera (the Arabic media) and the British Broadcasting Corporation (BBC).

It may also be helpful to read about or talk with soldiers who have fought in Afghanistan, Afghan civilians who have experienced the war, or members of humanitarian organizations who have worked there. Some of the organizations in the Organizations to Contact section may be able to put you in touch with people who have had direct experience in the Afghanistan war.

Identify the Issues Involved

Once you have gathered your information, review it methodically to discover the key issues involved. Why is the United States fighting in Afghanistan? Have US goals been achieved? Was it a war of necessity or choice? What is the role of Pakistan in this conflict? How has the increasingly widespread deployment of remote-controlled drones changed the nature of the war? How is the use of such technology perceived by Afghan civilians? By soldiers fighting there? How has modern communications technology, which allows soldiers to be in frequent contact with family and friends back home, changed the experience of the war, or the perceptions of those left behind? US soldiers in this war are experiencing higher rates of post-traumatic stress disorder and traumatic brain injury than ever before. How does that affect their lives when they return home, and what kind of support and treatment is available for them when they do return? How have strategy and tactics on both sides changed over the course of this long war? Have perceptions of the war on the part of soldiers, the US public, or the Afghan people changed over the course of the conflict? What has been the impact of media revelations of atrocities committed by some US soldiers? How has the relationship between the United States and Afghanistan evolved over time?

Evaluate Your Information Sources

In developing your own opinions, it is vital to evaluate the sources of the information you have discovered. Authors of books, magazine articles, and so forth, however well intentioned, have their own perspectives and biases that may affect how they present information on the subject. This is particularly true of a highly charged issue like war, which has such a high cost in lives lost and money spent.

Consider the authors' credentials and the organizations with which they are affiliated. They may offer information that is perfectly valid, but will present data and perspectives that support their viewpoint and that of their organization. For example, someone writing on behalf of the Department of Defense may emphasize possible threats to the very survival of the United States and promote the use of extreme measures and vast resources to counter them. Conversely, a member of a human rights organization may emphasize the impact of the war on the civilian population. On the other hand, if you find someone arguing against their expected bias—for example, a high-ranking military officer arguing against continuing the war in Afghanistan, or a human rights activist arguing in favor of some form of continuing military intervention—it may be worthwhile to pay particular attention to what they are saying. Always critically evaluate and assess your sources rather than take whatever they say at face value.

Examine Your Own Perspective

War is a complex and controversial topic. Spend some time exploring your own thoughts and feelings about it. Consider the attitudes and beliefs about war in general, or this war in particular, that you've received from family members, friends, and the media throughout your life. Such messages affect your own thoughts and feelings about the subject. If you or someone close to you has had direct experience of war, that may make it more challenging to form a clear view of the issues involved. On the other hand, it may give you special insight into the topic. Be aware of the tendency to look for perspectives and information that confirm what you already believe to be true, and to discount anything that contradicts your viewpoint. Counter this tendency by seeking out and seriously considering attitudes that differ from your own.

Form an Opinion and Take Action

Once you have gathered and organized information, identified the issues involved, and examined your own perspective, you will be ready to form an opinion on the war in Afghanistan, and to advocate that position in debates and discussions. Or perhaps you will decide that you cannot take a decisive position yet. In that case, ask yourself what you would need to know to make up your mind. Perhaps a bit more research would be helpful. Whatever position you take, be prepared to explain it clearly based on facts, evidence, and well-thought-out beliefs.

The editors have compiled the following list of organizations concerned with the issues debated in this book. The descriptions are derived from materials provided by the organizations. All have publications or information available for interested readers. The list was compiled on the date of publication of the present volume; names, addresses, phone and fax numbers, and e-mail and Internet addresses may change. Be aware that many organizations take several weeks or longer to respond to inquiries, so allow as much time as possible.

Afghanistan Analysts Network (AAN)
+93 (0)798 394167
e-mail: info@afghanistan-analysts.net
website: http://aan-afghanistan.com

The AAN is a nonprofit, independent policy research organization that aims to bring together the knowledge, experience, and drive of a large number of experts in the fields of Afghan politics, governance, rule of law, security, and regional affairs in order to better inform policy and increase the understanding of Afghan realities. In-depth reports are available on its website, such as "The International Community's Engagement in Afghanistan Beyond 2014" and "The Battle for Schools: The Taleban and State Education." The website also features blogs with commentary on events in Afghanistan and links to news reports on Afghanistan from around the world.

American Enterprise Institute (AEI)
1150 Seventeenth St. NW, Washington, DC 20036
(202) 862-5800 • fax: (202) 862-7177
e-mail: webmaster@aei.org
website: www.aei.org

The American Enterprise Institute is a private, nonpartisan, nonprofit institution dedicated to research and education on issues of government, politics, economics, and social welfare. It sponsors research and publishes materials to defend the principles of American freedom and democratic capitalism through projects such as its Center for Defense Studies. AEI publishes the bimonthly *American* and a series of papers in its Economic Outlook series. Various e-mail subscriptions are available on its website, including *AEI Today*, *National Security Outlook*, and *Critical Threats Quick Take*. Numerous articles about the war in Afghanistan can be found on its website, including "Five Disasters We'll Face if U.S. Retreats from Afghanistan" and "Stay the Course in Afghanistan."

Carnegie Endowment for International Peace (CEIP)
1779 Massachusetts Ave. NW
Washington, DC 20036
(202) 483-7600 • fax: (202) 483-1840
e-mail: info@carnegieendowment.org
website: carnegieendowment.org

The CEIP is a private, nonprofit organization dedicated to advancing cooperation between nations and promoting active international engagement by the United States. It publishes the quarterly journal *Foreign Policy*, a magazine of international politics and economics that is published in several languages and reaches readers in more than 120 countries. The CEIP also produces YouTube videos, hosts a Facebook page, and has a Twitter feed. A section on Afghanistan may be found under the heading "Regions" and includes content such as "Drones and IEDs: A Lethal Cocktail" and "Gambling on Reconciliation to Save a Transition: Perils and Possibilities in Afghanistan."

Cato Institute
1000 Massachusetts Ave. NW
Washington, DC 20001-5403
(202) 842-0200 • fax: (202) 842-3490
website: www.cato.org

The Cato Institute is a libertarian public policy research foundation dedicated to peace and limited government intervention in foreign affairs. It publishes numerous reports and periodicals, including *Policy Analysis* and *Cato Policy Review*, both of which discuss US policy in regional conflicts. Its website offers a searchable database of institute articles, news, and commentary, including podcasts and videos. Among the Cato Institute's many publications is the white paper *Escaping the "Graveyard of Empires": A Strategy to Exit Afghanistan*.

Central Intelligence Agency (CIA)
Office of Public Affairs, Washington, DC 20505
(703) 482-0623 • fax: (703) 482-1739
website: www.cia.gov

The CIA was created in 1947 with the signing of the National Security Act by President Harry S. Truman. The CIA seeks to collect and evaluate intelligence related to national security and to provide appropriate dissemination of such intelligence. Its website's Library section includes the popular publication *The World Factbook*, which provides information on the history, people, government, economy, geography, communications, transportation, military, and transnational issues for 267 world entities, including Afghanistan. Also notable is the "Kid's Page," which includes games and information resources for grades six–twelve.

Council on Foreign Relations
58 E. Sixty-Eighth St.
New York, NY 10065
(212) 434-9400 • fax: (212) 434-9800
website: www.cfr.org

The Council on Foreign Relations specializes in foreign affairs and studies the international aspects of American political and economic policies and problems. Its journal, *Foreign Affairs*, published five times a year, includes analysis of current conflicts around the world. Its website publishes editorials, interviews, articles, and videos. E-mail newsletters offered include *Daily News Brief,* the *World This Week,* and *Preventive Action Update.* Searching "Afghanistan" on the organization's website yields hundreds of results, including an interactive timeline of the US war in Afghanistan, as well as detailed background reports such as "The Taliban in Afghanistan" and "Afghanistan's National Security Forces."

Global Exchange
2017 Mission St., 2nd Fl.
San Francisco, CA 94110
(415) 255-7296 • fax: (415) 255-7498
e-mail: web@globalexchange.org
website: www.globalexchange.org

The human rights organization Global Exchange exposes economic and political injustice around the world. It supports education, activism, and a noninterventionist US foreign policy. Its "Stop Funding War" campaign seeks to inspire creative actions to expose the real cost of war at home and abroad, challenge war profiteering and military recruitment, and build people-to-people ties to expand understanding and tolerance. The organization's website offers a blog network, e-mail updates, and a section on ways to get involved. Its "Afghanistan" page includes background information, tips on getting involved, news updates, and links to additional resources.

The Heritage Foundation
214 Massachusetts Ave. NE, Washington, DC 20002-4999
(202) 546-4400
e-mail: info@heritage.org
website: www.heritage.org

Founded in 1973, the Heritage Foundation is a research and educational institute whose mission is to formulate and promote conservative public policies based on the principles of free enterprise, limited government, individual freedom, and a strong national defense. It publishes many books on foreign policy, such as *Winning the Long War*. Its website includes numerous articles about the war in Afghanistan.

Institute for Policy Studies (IPS)
1112 Sixteenth St. NW, Ste. 600, Washington, DC 20036
(202) 234-9382
e-mail: info@ips-dc.org
website: www.ips-dc.org

IPS is a think tank that acts as a policy and research resource for progressive movements such as the antiwar movement. IPS published *Ending the U.S. War in Afghanistan: A Primer*. A project of the IPS, Foreign Policy in Focus, connects research and actions of scholars, advocates, and activists seeking to make the United States a more responsible global partner. A variety of e-mail subscriptions are available, including *Unconventional Wisdom* and *Ideas into Action*. Numerous articles and commentaries on the war in Afghanistan are available on its website, including "Not the 'Good' War: Rethinking Afghanistan Eight Years Later" and "Learning from the Soviets in Afghanistan."

International Committee of the Red Cross
Washington Delegation (covers United States and Canada)
1100 Connecticut Ave. NW, Ste. 500
Washington, DC 20036
(202) 587-4600 • fax: (202) 587-4696
e-mail: was_washington@icrc.org
website: www.icrc.org

The International Committee of the Red Cross, more commonly known as simply the Red Cross, works to protect the lives and dignity of victims of war and civil violence. It directs and coordinates international relief activities and promotes humanitarian laws and principles. Its website includes the text of the Geneva Conventions, subsequent protocols, and articles and reports on recent issues related to its mission, including hundreds of articles about the war in Afghanistan, such as "Afghanistan: War-Hit Civilians Face Drought Risk" and "Afghanistan: 30 Years of Suffering."

United for Peace and Justice (UFPJ)
PO Box 607, Times Square Station
New York, NY 10108
(212) 868-5545
e-mail: info.ufpj@gmail.com
website: www.unitedforpeace.org

UFPJ opposes preemptive wars of aggression and rejects any drive to expand US control over other nations and strip Americans of rights at home under the cover of fighting terrorism and spreading democracy. The UFPJ website publishes news articles, essays, and information on recent antiwar events and has working groups focusing on specific issues such as Afghanistan. People can also sign up to receive *UFPJ Action Alerts*, which provide updates and ways to get involved in the work of the organization, member groups, and allies.

US Department of Defense (DoD)
1400 Defense Pentagon, Washington, DC 20301-1400
(703) 571-3343
website: www.defense.gov

The DoD is the federal government department that supervises all agencies of the government related to national security and the US Armed Forces. Among those agencies are the Departments of the Army, the Navy, and the Air Force, as well as the National Security Agency. Its website contains news releases, photo essays, and reports, including the reports *Progress Toward Security and Stability in Afghanistan—April 2011*, and *2011 National Military Strategy (02/08/2011)*. The DoD's website includes a special page on Afghanistan.

War Child North America
489 College St. West, Ste. 500
Toronto, ON M6G 1A5
CANADA
(416) 971-7474; toll-free: 1-866-WARCHILD
fax: (416) 971-7946

e-mail: info@warchild.ca
website: www.warchild.ca/

War Child's mission is to empower children and young people to flourish within their communities and overcome the challenges of living with, and recovering from, conflict. Its goals include increasing access to education, especially for girls and young women; creating a protective environment for the rights of children and youth; and ultimately working toward a world where no child knows war. Its website offers a newsletter, information on its programs in Afghanistan and other countries, and a section on how high school students can get involved.

Win Without War

1717 Massachusetts Ave. NW, Ste. 801, Washington, DC 20036
(202) 232-3317
e-mail: info@winwithoutwar.org
website: www.winwithoutwar.org

Win Without War is a forty-member coalition of organizations formed in 2002 to lead the first national campaign against the war in Iraq. Its current aims include working to demilitarize US policy in Afghanistan and to close the detention center at Guantánamo Bay. The organization's website features a blog, a Twitter feed, multimedia presentations, e-mail updates, and information sections on conflict in Afghanistan, Pakistan, Iraq, and Iran.

Women for Women International

4455 Connecticut Ave. NW, Ste. 200
Washington, DC 20008
(202) 737-7705 • fax: (202) 737-7709
e-mail: general@womenforwomen.org
website: www.womenforwomen.org

Women for Women International provides women survivors of war, civil strife, and other conflicts with the tools and resources to move from crisis and poverty to stability and self-sufficiency in order to promote viable civil societies. The organization's

"Afghanistan" page includes facts about Afghanistan, the impact of the war there, and how people can help improve the lives of women in Afghanistan. The website also offers reports such as *Strong Women Stronger Nations: 2009 Afghanistan Report*, and the quarterly newsletter *Outreach*.

BIBLIOGRAPHY

Books

Milo S. Afong, *Hunters: U.S. Snipers in the War on Terror*. New York: Berkley Caliber, 2010.

David A. Benhoff and Vincent J. Martinez, *Afghanistan, Alone & Unafraid*. Quantico, VA: Marine Corps University Press, 2010.

Eric Blehm, *The Only Thing Worth Dying For: How Eleven Green Berets Forged a New Afghanistan*. New York: HarperCollins, 2010.

Rusty Bradley and Kevin Maurer, *Lions of Kandahar: The Story of a Fight Against All Odds*. New York: Bantam, 2011.

Deborah Ellis, *Kids of Kabul: Living Bravely Through a Never-Ending War*. Toronto: Groundwood, 2012.

———, *Off to War: Voices of Soldiers' Children*. Toronto: Groundwood, 2008.

Dexter Filkins, *The Forever War*. New York: Knopf, 2008.

Brandon Friedman, *The War I Always Wanted: The Illusion of Glory and the Reality of War*. St. Paul, MN: Zenith, 2007.

Rafal Gerszak and Dawn Hunter, *Beyond Bullets: A Photo Journal of Afghanistan*. Toronto: Annick, 2011.

Ronald J. Glasser, *Broken Bodies, Shattered Minds: A Medical Odyssey from Vietnam to Afghanistan*. Palisades, NY: History, 2011.

Iraq Veterans Against the War and Aaron Glantz, *Winter Soldier, Iraq and Afghanistan: Eyewitness Accounts of the Occupations*. Chicago: Haymarket, 2008.

Ann Jones, *Kabul in Winter: Life Without Peace in Afghanistan*. New York: Picador, 2007.

Malalai Joya and Derrick Keefe, *A Woman Among Warlords: The Extraordinary Story of an Afghan Who Dared to Raise Her Voice*. New York: Scribner, 2011.

Sebastian Junger, *War*. New York: Twelve, 2010.

Daniele Mastrogiacomo, *Days of Fear: A Firsthand Account of Captivity Under the New Taliban*. New York: Europa Editions, 2010.

Suraya Sadeed and Damien Lewis, *Forbidden Lessons in a Kabul Guesthouse: The True Story of a Woman Who Risked Everything to Bring Hope to Afghanistan*. New York: Voice/Hyperion, 2011.

Benjamin Tupper, *Greetings from Afghanistan, Send More Ammo: Dispatches from Taliban Country*. New York: NAL Caliber, 2010.

Periodicals and Internet Sources

Afghanistan Study Group, "A New Way Forward: Rethinking U.S. Strategy in Afghanistan," August 16, 2010. www.afghani stanstudygroup.org/read-the-report/.

Mindy Belz, "Afghanistan 'Outside the Wire,'" *Weekly Standard*, February 6, 2012. www.weeklystandard.com/articles/afghanistan -outside-wire_618799.html.

Ross Caputi, "The Systemic Atrocity of Afghanistan's Occupation," *Guardian* (Manchester, UK), March 13, 2012. www.guardian .co.uk/commentisfree/cifamerica/2012/mar/13/systemic-atrocity -afghanistan-occupation.

C.J. Chivers, "A Changed Way of War in Afghanistan's Skies," *New York Times*, January 15, 2012. www.nytimes.com/2012/01/16 /world/asia/afghan-war-reflects-changes-in-air-war.html.

Patrick Cockburn, "Where War Goes, Propaganda Follows," *Independent* (London) February 11 2010. www.independent .co.uk/opinion/commentators/patrick-cockburn-where-war -goes-propaganda-follows-1895841.html.

Democracy Now!, "Behind the Afghan Massacre: Accused Soldier Suffered Brain Injury After Multiple Deployments in Iraq," March 14, 2012. www.democracynow.org/2012/3/14/behind _the_afghan_massacre_accused_soldier.

Jesse Ellison, "Afghanistan's War on Women Detailed in New Human-Rights Watch Report," Daily Beast, March 28, 2012. www.thedailybeast.com/articles/2012/03/28/afghanistan-s-war -on-women-detailed-in-new-human-rights-watch-report.html.

Colleen M. Getz, "Seeing a Fallen Soldier Home; Gratitude Should
   Be Foremost in American Hearts and Minds," *Washington Times*,
   May 30, 2010.

Glenn Greenwald, "The Causes of the Protests in Afghanistan,"
   Salon, February 26, 2012. www.salon.com/2012/02/26/the_
   causes_of_the_protests_in_afghanistan/.

Chris Hedges, "Murder Is Not an Anomaly in War," Truthdig,
   March 19, 2012. www.truthdig.com/report/item/murder_is_not
   _an_anomoly_in_war_20120319/.

Michael Hirsh, "The Disintegration of Obama's Afghanistan War
   Strategy," *Atlantic*, March 12, 2012. www.theatlantic.com/inter
   national/archive/2012/03/the-disintegration-of-obamas-afghan
   istan-war-strategy/254322/.

Xeni Jardin, "Inside Kabul: Landmine Survivor Aid Activist Live-
   Blogs from Lockdown in Afghanistan," Boing Boing, February
   28, 2012. http://boingboing.net/2012/02/28/inside-kabul-land
   mine-survivo.html.

Ann Jones, "Can Women Make Peace?," TomDispatch, January
   13, 2011. www.tomdispatch.com/blog/175340/tomgram%3A
   _ann_jones%2C_can_women_make_peace.

Sebastian Junger, "We're All Guilty of Dehumanizing the
   Enemy," *Washington Post*, January 13, 2012. www.washing
   tonpost.com/opinions/were-all-guilty-of-dehumanizing-the
   -enemy/2012/01/13/gIQAtRduwP_story.html.

William Kristol, "Men at War," *Weekly Standard*, January 23, 2012.
   www.weeklystandard.com/articles/men-war_616727.html.

Antony Loewenstein, "The Business of War in Afghanistan,"
   Al-Akhbar English, April 25, 2012. http://english.al-akhbar.com
   /content/business-war-afghanistan.

Luke Mogelson, "The Hard Way Out of Afghanistan," *New York
   Times*, February 1, 2012. www.nytimes.com/2012/02/05/maga
   zine/afghanistan.html.

Ronald E. Neumann, "U.S. troops Will Remain in Afghanistan
   Beyond 2014," *Washington Post*, February 19, 2012. www.wash

ingtonpost.com/opinions/us-troops-will-remain-in-afghanistan
-beyond-2014/2012/02/13/gIQA31xFOR_story.html.

Melissa Pritchard, "Finding Ashton/A Soldier's Story: US Women
Soldiers in Afghanistan," *O Magazine*, May 2010. http://www
.oprah.com/spirit/A-Soldiers-Story-US-Women-Soldiers-in
-Afghanistan_1

ProPublica, "Brain Wars: How the Military Is Failing Its Wounded,"
2011–2012. www.propublica.org/series/brain-wars.

Corinne Reilly, "A Chance in Hell," *Virginian-Pilot* (Hampton
Roads, VA), July 31, 2011. http://hamptonroads.com/achan
ceinhell.

Jeremy Schwartz, "Catastrophic Amputations Rise in Afghanistan
War's Final Years," *Austin (TX) Statesman*, February 18, 2012.
www.statesman.com/news/news/special-reports/catastrophic
-amputations-rise-in-afghanistan-war-1/nRkbq/.

Kim Sengupta, "War in Afghanistan: Mission Impossible?,"
Independent (London), March 28, 2012. www.independent
.co.uk/news/world/asia/war-in-afghanistan-mission-impossi
ble-7593595.html.

Jennifer Senior, "The Prozac, Paxil, Zoloft, Wellbutrin, Celexa,
Effexor, Valium, Klonopin, Ativan, Restoril, Xanax, Adderall,
Ritalin, Haldol, Risperdal, Seroquel, Ambien, Lunesta, Elavil,
Trazodone War," *New York*, February 14, 2011. http://nymag
.com/news/features/71277/.

David Smith-Ferri, "Above the Drone of War, Voices for Peace,"
Common Dreams, March 25, 2012. www.commondreams.org
/view/2012/03/25-7.

Yaroslav Trofimov, "Emboldened Taliban Try to Sell Softer Image,"
Wall Street Journal, January 28, 2012. http://online.wsj.com/arti
cle/SB10001424052970203806504577177074111336352.html.

Nick Turse, "Our Non-Withdrawal from Afghanistan," *Salon*,
February 13, 2012. www.salon.com/2012/02/13/our_non_with
drawal_from_afghanistan/singleton/.

Jere Van Dyk, "Losing the Media War in Afghanistan," CBS News, April 18, 2012. www.cbsnews.com/8301-503543_162 -57415874-503543/losing-the-media-war-in-afghanistan/.

Bing West, "Groundhog War: The Limits of Counterinsurgency in Afghanistan," *Foreign Affairs*, September/October 2011. www .foreignaffairs.com/articles/68133/bing-west/groundhog-war.

David Zucchino, "A Counterinsurgency Behind the Burka," *Los Angeles Times*, December 11, 2011. http://articles.latimes .com/2011/dec/11/nation/la-na-cultural-20111212.